SHADOWS OF AMBER

ALSO BY JOHN GREGORY BETANCOURT

Roger Zelazny's The Dawn of Amber

The Dawn of Amber
Chaos and Amber
To Rule in Amber

Roger Zelazny's Shadows of Amber

Shadows of Amber
Sword of Chaos (forthcoming)

Selected Fiction

The Blind Archer
Born of Elven Blood (with Kevin J. Anderson)
Cutthroat Island
Horizon (forthcoming from ibooks)
Johnny Zed
The Dragon Sorcerer
Rememory
Starskimmer
Star Trek Deep Space Nine: Devil in the Sky
Star Trek Deep Space Nine: The Heart of the Warrior
Star Trek The Next Generation: Double Helix, Book I: Infection
Star Trek Voyager: Incident at Arbuk

SHADOWS OF AMBER

BOOK FOUR IN THE "DAWN OF AMBER" SERIES

JOHN GREGORY BETANCOURT

ibooks

new york

DISTRIBUTED BY PUBLISHERS GROUP WEST

An Original Publication of ibooks, inc.

Copyright © 2005 Amber Ltd. Co.

An ibooks, inc. Book

ibooks, inc.
24 West 25th Street
New York, NY 10010

ISBN 1-59687-118-0

Edited by Howard Zimmerman

Jacket art by Aaron Campbell
Jacket design by Eric Goodman
Interior design by Gilda Hannah & John Betancourt
Typesetting by Wildside Press, LLC.

Printed in the U.S.A.

ACKNOWLEDGMENTS

The author would like to thank Theresa Thomas, L. Jagi Lamplighter, and Michael G. McGough for their help in reading early drafts and proofreading.

In memory of *Byron Preiss* (1952-2005)
whose vision and support made this book possible.

And for my wife *Kim*,
who makes all else possible.

ONE

ing Joslon cried, "Insults!" He pounded the beauti-
fully inlaid teak-and-mahogany conference table with
his fist. "Insults and yet more insults!" He quivered with
anger from the tip of his pointed gray beard to the
arches of his bushy gray eyebrows.

I found him almost comical, dressed in that intricately-embroi-
dered sea-green robe, but I suppressed my urge to laugh. No point in
adding to his imagined list of slights.

"You need to control your son," I said calmly, leaning back in my
chair. Playing a patient and reasonable king did not come easily, but I
could manage it if I had to. Kyar's rich farmlands could easily supply
my army with meat and grains for years to come.

With more patience than I really felt, I continued: "Let me re-
mind you that good relations between Amber and Kyar will benefit
both our peoples. For trust and friendship to grow between us, your
son must treat guests with proper respect. Like you, I *am* a king."

The ring on my right index finger pulsed twice sharply. A warning? I kept my expression neutral, but began to surreptitiously search
the room for any sign of danger. We were alone; where could the threat
come from?

"Respect?" Joslon leaned forward, mouth turning down and

deep-set eyes glaring. "You have received nothing *but* respect since your arrival! You abuse your position here, King Oberon —"

"Enough." I shoved back my chair and stood. "Listen well, Joslon," I said in a low but earnest voice. I leaned forward across the table, towering over him. "Prince Adric *insulted* me. He called me a coward and challenged me to a duel. I *will* fight him. If he ends the duel at first blood, honor will be satisfied."

"You will kill him! I will lose my favorite son!"

"I want him alive as much as you do because this treaty is important to me. To *Amber*. This will be your last chance to sign it. My patience is at an end."

Joslon leaned back, jaw set stubbornly. "Then do not duel my son."

"I cannot let insults pass unanswered. My honor — the honor of Amber — demands satisfaction."

My ring pulsed again, more urgently than before. What did it mean? I tightened my right hand into a fist, running my thumb along the spikard's smooth gold surface.

Casually I began to pace, letting my attention wander the room. Intricate frescoes covered every wall, showing detailed forest scenes. The high beamed ceiling held a wrought-iron chandelier, in which two dozen thick tallow candles burned. Heavy carpets covered the floors. I saw no sign of danger anywhere, but my ring had never been wrong before. Could it sense assassins sent by the king's son?

Joslon placed his hands carefully on the table and stood. Behind him, I noticed the wall bulging slowly in toward us, like a water-skin filling up — a neat trick, since the wall behind the fresco was made of heavy plaster. Magic? I chewed my lip thoughtfully. This had to be what the ring wanted to warn me about.

"Leave," the king said in a heavy voice. He pointed dramatically toward the door. "Depart my lands. I will have nothing more to do with you — or with Amber!"

I drew my sword. "Get out of this room," I said, watching the wall behind him. I had a very bad feeling about it.

King Joslon recoiled in fear. "You *dare* to raise a weapon against *me*, in my own castle?"

"Do as I say, Joslon!" I pointed with the tip of my sword. The wall behind him began to crack. Dust and chips of painted plaster fell silently to the floor. "Take a look!"

He stared at me blankly. "What —"

"I have no time for your squawking. Something big is coming . . . big and very dangerous. If you want to live, you had better get out of this room, and you had better do it now!"

Instead of running for his life, though, he turned and stared — a huge mistake, and his last. Heavy stone blocks suddenly spewed outward from the bulging wall, striking him in his head and his chest. He fell with a shriek, and I lost sight of him beneath the débris and roiling cloud of dust.

A hole ten feet high and fifteen feet wide now gaped before me. Inside lay an unnatural darkness that seemed to suck the color from everything around us. It radiated a numbing cold. My breath began to mist in the air.

The ring on my finger tightened painfully. When something in the darkness *moved*, every fiber of my body screamed, "Run!" But I forced myself to stand and watch. I had to know more. I couldn't just leave — not without seeing whatever lay inside.

Part of that darkness stretched, *reached*. Like the tentacle of a squid, only blunt and featureless, a thick black limb thrust into the conference room. Quickly, I retreated toward the door. The limb had an oddly murky, nearly translucent quality, almost like smoke or fog. And the cold grew worse, a bone-freezing, life-sucking chill like nothing I had ever felt before.

What *was* that thing? My eyes never left it. Even when I bumped up against the door, I kept staring.

Tentatively at first, like a man probing the space where a pulled tooth had been, the limb turned this way and that. It seemed to be blindly exploring . . . or seeking something. *Me?*

"What do you want?" I demanded. My voice rang out in the silence. Could it hear me? Was it intelligent?

Extending slowly, the limb passed like a ghost through the teak-and-mahogany conference table. As it did, the wood turned gray and fell to dust. Still the limb advanced on my position.

I reached back and grasped the door's latch. How could I possibly defend against *that*? It had passed through the table! Would a sword even cut it? Somehow, I didn't think so.

"Answer me!" I said loudly, lifting the latch. Best to make a strategic retreat for now . . . at least until I found out more about it. "What do you want?"

No reply.

Yanking open the door, I backed out into the castle's great hall, then kicked the door shut. That slamming noise echoed far too loudly. Then the latch fell into place with an audible *click*. Hopefully the creature wouldn't figure out how I'd disappeared — at least, not for a few more minutes. That would give me time to gather up my brother and return to Amber.

"King Oberon?" a quavering voice called from behind me. "What have you done?"

Laoni, Joslon's head minister, had spotted me, of course. Realizing how suspicious everything must look to him, I winced inwardly. How could I have left the conference room with a drawn sword in hand? *Stupid, stupid, stupid!* They would all think I'd murdered their king. Why didn't anything ever go as planned?

When I glanced around the hall, I found dozens of servants and retainers, not to mention the king's advisors and a half a dozen guards, staring at me with horrorstruck expressions. I put on a smile anyway. Maybe they would think I had made some joke for Joslon's benefit, or shown the king my weapon.

Laughing, as if I'd made some great jest, I sheathed my sword.

"Oberon?" my brother Conner said.

He stood in a quiet alcove to the right. Short like our father, and with our father's dark intense eyes, he had been talking with Laoni and several other ministers while I met with the king.

With more confidence than I felt, I crossed over to them. Conner wore green as usual, a rich forest-dark shirt laced at the neck, with black pants and boots. A large emerald ring on his right index finger glinted as it caught the light.

Conner's eyebrows raised slightly. *Trouble?* asked his eyes. Almost casually, he dropped one hand to the hilt of his own sword. Though slight of build, he was quite skilled with a blade. He would account well for himself if we had to fight our way out of the castle.

Subtly, I shook my head. I hadn't done anything wrong; we didn't need to fight — at least, not yet. And I wanted to stay long enough to learn more about this creature.

"What happened to the king?" Laoni demanded. He was a fair man, in my opinion, honest but demanding. I had come to respect him over the last few days.

"King Joslon has thrown me out," I said with a frown. "I have been ordered to leave Kyar immediately. Send someone to the stables. I want our horses saddled and waiting. We're going home."

"Give us a minute to confer with his majesty," said Laoni hastily. "Perhaps things are not quite as bad as you think —"

"It won't do any good," I said. With King Joslon dead, Prince Adric would assume the throne, and Adric seemed more inclined to execute me than to continue trade negotiations. I had no doubt he would blame me for his father's death.

And he might have been right. I had the oddest feeling that the creature had come for me, not King Joslon. Someone — or something — had sent it.

Laoni clearly hadn't believed my story. He drew the other two ministers aside, and they huddled together, frowning and muttering and casting uneasy glances in my direction. None seemed happy at the prospect of our departure — after all, trade would have benefited Kyar as much as Amber, maybe more so. And yet they understood King Joslon's position. Events of the previous night *had* been nothing short of disastrous, after all . . .

Yet, to be fair, how was *I* to know Prince Adric's wife would sneak into my bed after the evening banquet? I had done nothing to encourage Lady Miana's attentions. Quite the contrary, in fact — I had spent the evening flirting with several buxom serving girls, any one of whom would have satisfied me. Nor had it been my fault that Miana had been discovered on her way out of my chambers several hours later by no less a personage than Prince Adric himself. Since she looked sweaty and disheveled and more deeply satisfied than she must have been in years, Prince Adric had jumped to conclusions.

Yes, there had been poor judgment on everyone's part. Not that I could blame Lady Miana for preferring my company to Prince Adric's, of course, but still . . .

"About our horses?" I said.

Laoni started for the door to the conference room. "One moment while I confer with His Majesty, Lord Oberon!" he called.

For a heartbeat I debated the wisdom of warning him about the creature. Just as I opened my mouth to call him back, Prince Adric stormed into the hall with six more guards in tow. Adric was shorter version of his father, with the same sallow complexion, a sharp-pointed black beard, and muddy brown eyes. Unlike his father, though, his thin lips twisted back perpetually in a cruel sneer.

"What did you do to my father?" he demanded, staring up at me — I was a good head and a half taller.

When he drew a short, curved sword, I almost laughed. I had knives longer than his blade. The guards behind him did the same, however.

"Nothing," I said. I crossed my arms and stared him straight in the eye.

"You came out of that conference room with your sword drawn, demanding horses. If those aren't the actions of a murderer —"

"Shouldn't you check on the king," I said, smiling through my teeth, "rather than blather on about it outside the door? And when you're done checking on him, I expect an apology!"

His sneer turned into a hate-filled glare. "If you have hurt him," he said, a faint quaver in his already shrill voice, "you will never leave Kyar alive! I swear it by the Six Ruthless Gods!"

TWO

I jerked my head toward the conference chamber. "Go in and see for yourself." Its door had turned faintly gray at the center, but Adric was too busy hating me to notice. "A creature got loose inside. That's why I drew my sword — to protect myself. I barely got out."

He snarled, "You must think me a fool!"

I bit back the obvious retort. Instead, with a lightly mocking tone, I replied: "See for yourself, O Prince. I'll wait here until you're done." Or done in.

"Watch him," he said sharply to the guards. "Don't let him run." Turning, he stomped over to the conference room, glaring at me the entire time.

Truly, he deserved whatever he got.

I put a hand on Conner's shoulder, steering him a few feet away from the ministers so we could talk without being overheard.

"An animal?" Conner said doubtfully. Clearly he didn't believe me, either.

"That's the truth — a magical creature of some kind. It broke through the stone wall behind the king."

"Why didn't you kill it?"

"Because it's huge, black, and colder than ice — and it passes

17

through solid objects like a ghost, destroying them. My sword would-n't have touched it."

"But you drew it anyway."

"Hell, yes! If I'm going to die, it will be with a sword in my hand!"

"Ah." His brow furrowed as concern mingled with curiosity. "You didn't summon it somehow, did you?"

"Of course not. I don't know why, but I got the feeling it was stalking me. Someone *sent* it."

He looked at the prince. "Adric, maybe? Murder the king, inherit the throne, and blame you?"

"He's far too stupid. Look at him! He has no idea what he's get-ting into."

Still watching me rather than the door, Adric rapped loudly with the hilt of his sword and called for his father. All six guards had half turned now to watch him. I found I was holding my breath, too.

Conner continued, "Who in Kyar wants you dead besides Prince Adric, anyway? His wife?"

"Hardly!" I chuckled. "She begged me to take her back to Am-ber!"

"Who else, then?" Conner said.

"Maybe someone who isn't from Kyar. Half of the Courts of Chaos want me dead, after all, and you can put King Swayvil at the top of the list. He could easily send creatures like that one after me, if he wanted to."

"Perhaps."

"You don't sound convinced," I said.

"This doesn't feel like something Swayvil would do."

"Father?" Adric called a second time. He pounded on the door more loudly. "Are you hurt? Father?"

I shrugged. "Who else, then?"

"I don't know." Conner frowned, eyes distant. "Well, look on the bright side."

"There's a bright side?"

"It was time for us to leave Kyar anyway. King Joslon wasn't going to sign a treaty with you. His ministers as much as admitted it."

"A pity." I sighed. So much wasted time . . .

Conner dropped his hand to the hilt of his sword again. "You take the three guards on the right and I'll take the three on the left. You can have Adric, too — not that he'll give you much of a fight. We can reach the stables before the castle guard turns out."

"Feeling bloodthirsty today?"

"Merely annoyed. Mostly at the prince."

"Hold on for now. I want you to see that creature. Maybe you'll recognize it."

He nodded. "Fair enough. Then we kill them all!"

When I laughed, Adric's glare intensified. He probably thought I'd made some joke at his expense.

To Conner, I said, "We'll have more to worry about from the creature than the guards. We may have to leave faster than that."

"A Trump?"

"Yes."

Casually I eased open the pouch at my belt. Inside sat a deck of magical cards called Trumps. If we needed a quick exit from Kyar, they were our best bet. The top card showed a woodland scene with a castle on a hill in the background: Amber. *Home.* We could be back there in just a few heartbeats.

I eased out the Trump and held it face-down in the palm of my hand, feeling its cool ivory texture, sensing the power its image contained.

"Father?" Adric called loudly. "I'm coming in —"

He reached for the door's latch.

"How dangerous *is* this creature?" Conner asked.

"Its arrival blew out a heavy stone wall. Then its touch turned the conference table into dust. Take a quick look when Adric opens the door, then we'll go."

"I don't like running away."

"I don't, either. So call it a strategic retreat instead." I had learned the phrase from our father; he had become a master of such military maneuvers over the years. Run away, and stab your enemies in the back another day, when they're distracted. "Sometimes it's the only wise thing to do."

We both watched Adric expectantly. Still glaring at me, he lifted the latch and pulled.

The entire door crumbled. A cold, black, foglike limb darted out of the opening and passed *through* the prince's chest.

The creature sucked the life out of him. There was no other way to describe it. His hair turned bone-gray. He drew a short, gasping breath. Then, as the skin pulled tight across his skull, he fell slowly to one side. When he hit the floor, his body disintegrated. Even his clothes turned to dust.

Panic erupted throughout the room. Most of the women fled, shrieking. The servants ran wildly, shouting for help.

Screaming their fiercest battle-cries, Adric's guards charged the creature with drawn weapons. One threw a knife, which passed through the black limb as though it weren't there. Then they were on top of it, slashing wildly, but they might have been fighting fog for all the damage their weapons did.

"Do you know what it is?" I asked Conner over the tumult.

"I don't know — and I don't want to find out! I've never seen or heard of anything like it!"

Gyrating wildly, the black limb grazed one, then another of the guards. In seconds, four of them died as horribly as their master.

Panting, cursing, calling on a dozen different deities for aid, the remaining two backed out of its reach. Still they refused to flee — I gave them credit for bravery. Anyone less well trained would have run away by this point.

Distantly, a gong began to sound. I looked around quickly. Laoni and the other ministers had all disappeared — perhaps they had raised the alarm. Far-off I heard voices calling questions, giving orders, demanding answers. I thought I heard my own name more than once. Doubtless they thought I had set this creature loose in the castle, and I couldn't blame them for reaching that conclusion.

Like a cobra, the black limb rose up, weaving back and forth in the air. It seemed to be searching for something . . . or someone.

Me?

When it turned in my direction, I knew.

"Time to go," I said. I raised my Trump — but still I hesitated.

21

Could I learn anything more about this fog-creature? What if it came after me again?

More guards poured into the hall. I tensed, one hand dropping to my sword's hilt, but they rushed the monster instead of me — and died by the dozens.

"Oberon . . ." Conner said, a warning note in his voice. "Let's get out of here!"

"Okay," I said.

Quickly, I raised the Trump. I didn't think we could learn anything else right now, anyway.

Before I could use the Trump, though, the whole of Castle Kyar jolted and shook. It felt as though something huge had shifted beneath the foundations. How large *was* this creature?

At that point, the three remaining guards threw down their swords and fled. The tendril paused a second, but rather than pursue them, it started for me.

"Hurry!" said Conner.

I stared hard at the card and its image of a lush green forest. Colors deepened. A breeze ripe with the scents of earth and leaves and growing things touched my face. From the trees, I heard songbirds warbling. Then the scene expanded to fill the whole of my vision, vibrant and real.

I stepped forward into it, dragging Conner along. When I lowered the card, we stood side by side at the edge of a deep forest. The sun stood almost directly overhead; it had to be just about noon.

Home.

Safe.

I took a deep breath, lowered the card, and let myself relax. Even if we walked the whole way, we would still reach the castle in time for lunch.

My one regret was not being able to take Lady Miana back here with us. Still, she ought to be safe now; the creature had been after me. Why would it stay to destroy Kyar?

Turning, I gazed up the sharply sloped hill — almost a small mountain — upon which Castle Amber perched. Scaffolding still covered the outer walls, where masons continued their work. It had been three years since construction began on the castle, and it would be at least three more before it finished. But it would be one of the greatest buildings ever constructed, with thick walls, lavish halls, and room enough for every member of my family, no matter how numerous we became. Not that we had very many left right now, thanks to King Swayvil . . .

The ring on my index finger slowly relaxed its grip; I felt pins and needles from returning circulation. I hadn't realized how hard it had tightened.

"Thanks," I said to it quietly. I didn't know if it understood me, but it couldn't hurt to express my gratitude. It might well have saved my life — and not for the first time.

Conner was trembling slightly. The creature must have disturbed and frightened him more than I'd realized.

"Do you have *any* idea where that thing might have come from?" I asked. "Is it a creature of Chaos?"

I could easily see King Swayvil sending it to kill me; before seizing the throne, Swayvil had spent years tracking down members of our family, trying to destroy our bloodline . . . and mostly succeeding.

"I don't know," he said slowly. He seemed to shake off the fear that had overtaken him. "I never saw anything like it before. You'd better ask Freda. Or Dad, if he's feeling cooperative."

"Hah!" Our father never cooperated with anyone, unless it suited his own grand designs. "Freda it is, then."

I started up a narrow, winding trail more suited for goats than people. Our sister knew a lot about magic; if anyone besides our father could put a name to that thing, it would be her.

Then the ring on my finger suddenly tightened. Another warning? I drew up short and looked around, a bad feeling rising inside.

The trees to our left, in the thickest part of the forest, began to bulge and distort. It reminded me of the wall in the conference room just before the creature burst through.

"It's coming!" I said. Involuntarily, I shivered.

"Impossible!" Conner said.

"It's following us!"

"But how? You used a Trump! It shouldn't be able to get here!"

"Maybe it can follow magical trails through Shadow." I thought fast. Assuming it traveled the same way as before, we still had a minute or two before it broke into this world. That gave us time for . . . what? Reinforcements? Running away again? Something else?

We needed a way to defeat it. Maybe Dad or Freda could think of something. I certainly couldn't.

To Conner I said, "Run to Castle Amber — don't risk a Trump in case the creature can use it to follow you — and see if anyone knows what it is and how to kill it." I turned to face the bulging trees. "I know it's after me. I'll lead it away. As soon as someone figures out how to destroy it, use a Trump and let me know."

"Right!"

Without another word, Conner turned and sprinted up the trail toward the castle. Good man: follow instructions now, ask questions later.

I took a deep breath. No time to waste.

I ran straight for the creature.

THREE

en feet from the bulging trees, I veered aside and followed the line of the forest, plowing through waist-high grass and weeds, leaping a small stream, skirting tangles of thornbush and honeysuckle. If this creature needed an actual human scent to follow, it would now catch mine rather than Conner's. Hopefully that would be enough to bring it after me.

Two hundred yards away, I paused and looked over my shoulder. At that moment, branches and tree trunks burst outward into splinters. Something large and black and nearly shapeless moved half behind the cover of the forest, half in the open. Rounded black limbs reached a hundred feet into the sky. More limbs stretched from the forest at ground level, toward me. At their touch, bushes and trees lost their leaves, turned gray, and collapsed in puffs of dust. Grass withered and died. The stream froze. Even as far away as I now stood, I felt a sharp coldness radiating from its darkly massive body.

Then it paused as if confused. Some tendrils turned in the direction Conner had gone, some toward me.

I picked up a fist-sized rock and threw it. It passed through the center of the creature without doing any damage.

"Hey!" I shouted. Waving my arms, I jumped up and down, trying to get its attention. It had to follow me, not my brother. "Over here! *Hey!*"

That did it. A pair of tendrils moved slightly toward me, paused, moved again. Did it have eyes? Could it see me? Three of the overhead limbs stretched in my direction, and it started to move toward me — it had located its prey.

"Come on! Come and get me!" I shouted. As long as I kept it away from the castle, my family would be safe. Hopefully Dad and Freda would think of a way to kill it soon!

Rippling faintly now, the black mass oozed quickly toward me, destroying hundreds of trees in the process; they simply disappeared as it engulfed them. The bulk of the creature had to be twenty feet high and forty feet wide.

I had half expected it to rise up and walk on those long black limbs, but it pulled them into the main mass of its body and rolled or glided in my direction.

Turning, I began to run. Every minute or so, I glanced over my shoulder.

Moving faster now, it flowed toward me, cutting a broad, bleak highway across the land. At this rate, it would catch up with me in a couple of minutes.

"Come on, Conner!" I muttered. "What's taking so long?"

Tucking down my head, I ran on tirelessly. My breath surged; my legs pounded. As I ran, I began to shift myself into different Shadow-worlds. The waist-high grass yielded up a deer trail, which made running easier. A hint of mauve in the sky . . . an unexpected turn in the path . . . a boulder as large as a house, behind which stood a saddled black stallion . . .

I knew that horse well. I had ridden its twins dozens of times through Shadows. In one bound I leaped into the saddle, kicked him to a gallop, and headed down a trail that now widened into a proper road.

Craning my neck, I looked back.

Big mistake. It was still gaining on me. Now that it had my scent, that oozing blackness flowed across the land with the speed of a wildfire, still destroying trees and brush and grass. Nothing seemed to slow it down.

Time to change that.

Crouching lower, I urged the stallion to greater speed. As his legs churned powerfully, beating a steady rhythm on the stone of the highway, I shifted us through Shadows. The sky took on a deeper azure. The road narrowed, five feet wide, then four, then three. To either side, marshy quicksands began to bubble; the stink of marsh gas grew thick and unwholesome.

Then the road grew brittle, cracking under the stallion's iron-shod hooves. When I glanced back, I saw bits of broken stone sinking slowly into the softly bubbling waters.

Let the creature follow me now!

The road grew wide and firm again. I reigned in the stallion, and we stood still, panting for the moment. The ring on my finger tightened painfully. Clearly it didn't want me to stop.

The creature reached the edge of the marsh, following the road. Without hesitation, it rolled across the water, heading straight for me.

It didn't sink.

It didn't even slow down.

Cursing, I wheeled the stallion around and kicked him to a gallop again. That hadn't worked. What else could I try? Rain? Hail? Lightning?

Over the next two hours, I thundered across rain-swept grasslands, sun-baked deserts, and icy tundra. Burning winds blasted the shadow-creature. Lightning bolts struck it, sandstorms scoured it, then hailstones the size of cattle pounded its body.

Nothing stopped it.

Nothing even slowed it down.

If anything, it seemed to be growing *larger*, as if it fed on everything I threw its way.

I changed to a fresh horse more than a dozen times and kept running. Finally, as we crossed a vast glacier, the thing showed the first sign of weakness . . . it slowed slightly, and I began to pull ahead. Once more I changed mounts, and I spent the rest of the afternoon riding hard across an endless expanse of ice.

And still it followed.

Hours stretched, threatening to become days. I continued to change horses more times than I could count, and the chase continued.

Would it never give up? I looked back over my shoulder. This creature seemed as tireless as the wind. Once more I racked my brain for ideas. What would stop it? What could I throw against it?

Finally, when I had all but given up hope, I felt a light mental touch at the back of my mind — someone trying to contact me through a Trump. About time, too.

Giving my horse free rein to run, I concentrated on whoever was trying to reach me.

The image of my sister Freda appeared. She wavered, faint and uncertain, so far away we could barely hear each other.

"Where are you?" she asked. "Are you safe?"

"I'm ten minutes ahead of that creature!" I cried. "I've tried every trick I can think of to slow it down, but it's still coming! Did you talk to Dad? Do you know what it is? Can we stop it?"

"It was not born of Chaos," she said. "I saw it from the castle walls. Father believes the Feynim may have sent it."

"What?" I said in surprise. The Feynim were strange, unworldly creatures born of an ancient power other than Chaos or Amber — something older and nearly incomprehensible to us. According to my father, they had many names . . . the fey, shrikers, elves. I knew they sometimes walked through Shadows, observing us and our actions, but I had never known them to interfere before — let alone attack someone.

And why attack *me*? I had never done anything to them before. It didn't make sense!

Freda went on, "Father disappeared into his workshop. He may be trying to help you . . . but do not count on him."

"I never do," I said. "Did he say anything at all?"

"He called you a fool."

"Anything *useful*?"

"Something about a new move in the game . . ."

"Not that again!" Dad had been acting crazier than usual since he had drawn the Pattern. At times, he tended to rant about our all being pawns in some vast cosmic game. I didn't have much tolerance for such nonsense at the best of times.

But could he be right? Could this creature have been sent by the Feynim?

As far as I knew, the Feynim considered my family insignificant . . . more amusing than threatening. The one time we had asked them for help against Chaos, they had refused to get involved, acting if not exactly *friendly*, at least neutral toward us. One had even given me the spikard I now wore as a ring on my finger.

So why attack us? It didn't make sense.

"Oberon," my sister said, "Father may be right. I think the fey may have sent it."

"What makes you think so?" I said.

"There are legends about creatures like the one chasing you," she said. "Long ago, when the armies of Chaos invaded the Feynim worlds, the Feynim sent creatures against us. Those creatures sound a lot like the one chasing you now."

"That's interesting," I said, "but how do I kill it?"

"I don't know."

"What did the armies of Chaos do?"

"They were slaughtered. Tens of thousands of our best men died. It was a devastating rout. We never again invaded the Feynim worlds."

"Great. So I'm just supposed to roll over and die, is that it?"

"Of course not!" She hesitated.

"You thought of something!" I said.

"It is just an idea . . ."

"Tell me! I'm desperate!"

"Stop running blindly," she said. "Return to the Pattern. It is a place of great power. Draw on its strength. Use its power to defend yourself."

"But *how*?"

"You know the Pattern better than any of us — even Father. It is part of you."

"That's not much help!"

"And Oberon . . . good luck . . ." Her image faded.

I shook my head, returning to the *here* and *now*. My horse began to stumble. Quickly, I shifted to another Shadow, where a fresh mount waited around a curve in the trail. Once more we began to gallop, just holding our own ahead of the creature.

Maybe Freda did have the right idea. Running certainly wasn't helping.

What *would* happen if I lead the creature to the Pattern? If Freda was mistaken, if I couldn't somehow defeat it there, setting it loose at the heart of our universe might destroy everything we had worked for in the last three years.

And yet — did I have a choice? How much longer could I last, running headlong through Shadows? What other options remained?

I glanced back. The creature had nearly caught up while I talked to my sister. Urging my horse to greater effort, we pulled a little bit ahead.

Though stronger and faster than any normal man, I still had my limits. True exhaustion lay another five or six hours ahead, but I had already begun to tire from the chase. If I didn't do something soon, the creature would catch me. It was inevitable.

I knew the risks of leading the creature to the Pattern. Three years ago, I had helped my father destroy a flawed version of the Pattern. I had watched as an entire universe collapsed. Only when a new Pattern had been inscribed did order return . . . for the correct Pattern cast an infinite number of Shadows, each its own world with its own people.

If anything happened to the new Pattern, my world — and everything I had ever known — would cease to exist.

Bringing this dark creature to the Pattern seemed like a mad, impossible idea. And yet, what else could I do? My sister's instincts toward magic often proved right. I would have to trust her and hope for the best.

At least I could stall its arrival at the Pattern to give myself time to rest and recover. Time ran at different speeds in different Shadows; hours in Amber might be days or minutes in other worlds. Luckly I knew a world where minutes seemed like hours to the rest of the universe . . .

With that Shadow fixed in my mind, I rode hard, letting the land shift and change around me. Ice to forest to grasslands . . . mountains to gently rolling hills dotted with grazing snargs . . . night, blissful and slumbering . . . desert spotted with scraggly, skeletal plants . . .

Finally I reached my destination. Here, two pumpkin-colored moons hung low in a deep-purple sky studded with stars. By the moons' orange glow, I reigned in my horse and paused to gaze across this barren, desolate land. A low, moaning wind carried the strange, rich, spicy scents of desert plants.

Nothing had changed; this place remained exactly as I had remembered.

The creature, still behind me, showed no sign of slowing. I had two or three minutes before it would catch up . . . but with the time difference between this Shadow and Amber, that left me with an hour or more at the Pattern . . . enough time to walk its length and prepare myself for battle.

I steered my horse into a ravine. The stallion trembled from exhaustion, his sides flecked with foam and sweat. When I dismounted and slapped his rump, he trotted off alone. Without me on his back, he should be safe enough here.

Then, taking a deep breath, I drew out my deck of Trumps. I picked through them until I found the one I wanted . . . an image of the Pattern, the huge magical symbol at the center of the universe, as painted by my father. The graceful, sweeping lines glowed with a clear blue light.

My father had traced the Pattern on an enormous slab of rock with his lifeblood. Even in a picture, it radiated power.

I raised the card, stared at it, felt it coming to life before me. This had better work.

Taking a deep breath, I stepped forward —

— and emerged into daylight. I blinked into the brightness. Here the air tasted crisp and fresh. Every leaf on every tree stood straight and still, as though made of deep green glass. You could not have asked for a more perfect day or a more perfect setting.

Turning, I faced the Pattern. Energy seemed to ripple off its sleek lines, coming in waves across the whole vast and intricate design.

I breathed deeply, enjoying the sensation. I had not been here in almost a year, and it felt good to return. Every time I saw it, the Pattern filled me with a strange, almost intoxicating sense of power. The nearer I came to it, the stronger I felt its pull.

Here . . . yes, I could face the creature here. No — better to be standing in the center of the Pattern, where I would be most attuned to its presence and could draw upon its energy.

Without hesitation, I set foot on the glowing blue line where the Pattern began. Here my father had first begun to trace it with his blood. As my boot touched down, my vision flickered and my body began to tingle. I expected that; I had felt the same sensation every time I had walked the Pattern's length.

Another step, and a needling pain shot through my skull. Another, and blood pounded in my temples. Another, and my eyes began to ache.

Traveling its length was never an easy task — but each time the journey had grown a little less hard. Knowing what to expect helped.

I pressed on. The trick was to never stop, never hesitate, and keep your goal in mind. I would get there eventually. It might be difficult, it might be painful, but I knew I could do it.

Once more the Pattern seemed to radiate power in waves. A giddiness ran through me; I felt buoyant in a way I couldn't properly explain. I forced another step, then another.

Then everything grew hard. Head bent, I concentrated on lifting one foot at a time, moving it forward, and setting it down. With each step, strange and unpleasant jolts shot up my legs and into my thighs, like walking on some prickly carpet.

One step, then another.

Keep walking.

One step, then another.

I followed the path as it curved into a series of long and graceful sweeps. It was easier here. Of course, I knew every twist and turn already; I could see them forever branded into my mind even when I closed my eyes. Blindfolded, I could have followed the Pattern without missing a single step.

When I entered the first curve, walking grew hard again. My legs dragged; I had to pick up each foot and put it down through sheer will-power. Bright blue sparks swirled up around my feet, then up to my knees; every hair on my body stood at attention.

Never stop.

Never hesitate.

One step at a time.

One step, then another, then another.

Walking got easier at the end of the curve, and I let out my breath in one huge gasp. My head pounded. Sweat drenched my body, dripping from my chin and nose and soaking my shirt. I had only come a third of the way. Why did it seem so much harder this time?

After a brief period of easiness, where I moved quickly, sparks once again swirled, this time up to my waist. It felt as though I slogged through mud.

Another step.

Never hesitate.

Another step.

One foot at a time.

My legs went numb. Then, as the numbness spread to my chest, I had to force myself not only to walk, but to breathe. I knew I could do this thing; I had done it three times before.

Rounding the curve, the numbness passed and I could breathe easier once more. Blue sparks ghosted across my body like thousands of ants. I ignored them; they were a distraction, harmless.

Keep moving.

Halfway there.

I pressed on, ever on. The blue line of the Pattern curved back upon itself, then straightened. I could barely move now; progress seemed impossibly slow, inches at a time.

The end grew near. The hair on my neck and arms rose again. I had to force each foot forward. If I stopped, I didn't think I would be able to start again.

The path curved sharply, and all of a sudden I found I could walk almost normally. Gathering my strength, I strode forward as quickly as I could, but then a heaviness began to grow on me. Once more I found it harder and harder to advance, as though chains now dragged on my arms and legs and chest. I might have been pulling a ten-ton weight.

I pressed forward.

One step.

A second.

A third.

Each took more effort than the last. When I raised my hand, sparks poured like water from my skin.

Through!

Suddenly I could walk again. Sparks dashed and flew all around me. I felt hot and cold, wet and dry, and my eyes burned with a fire that could not be quenched. I blinked hard many times.

One more curve.

Almost there.

Dizzy, I reeled through another turn, a short one this time. Then straight, then another curve.

The last part was the hardest yet. I could barely move, barely see, barely breathe. My skin froze, then boiled. Sparks blinded me. The very universe seemed to beat down upon my head and shoulders.

I concentrated on one foot at a time. As long as I kept moving, I drew closer to my goal. Just another inch at a time — then another — anything to keep going —

Now I could scarcely see the Pattern. Barely able to breathe, I used the last of my strength to take the final step.

Then I was done. I had made it to the center!

Gasping for air, I bent double and tried to catch my breath. How much time did I have? How long until the creature came?

Rising, still panting, I looked around. Trees, tall and silent, surrounded the slab of rock upon which I stood. There were no birds, no insects, no animals of any kind. My own rough breathing was the only sound that broke the absolute stillness, sounding too loud and out of place.

Poised.

Waiting.

If any world could possibly be safe from the creature, this would be it. Here, at the heart of the Pattern from which all Shadows fell, lay the cornerstone of my family's power . . . of *my* power.

I drew a deep breath. I felt strong. Ready.

Shadows of Amber

"Just try to get me now!" I whispered.

The ring on my finger tightened.

To my right, I noticed the trees beginning to bulge.

FOUR

closed my eyes and focused all my attention on the Pattern. I held it in my head, every line and nuance, every curve and curl. It was part of me, just as I was part of it. We were one.

A strange calmness settled across my mind. I heard the trees burst apart with a sound of splintering wood. And it seemed to me I gazed down on this spot from a remote time and place. Every movement felt familiar, an intricate dance I had performed many times before . . . that I would perform many times again.

I opened my eyes.

Splinters of wood rained down across the land. I did not flinch, did not move at all. A few hit the immense stone slab upon which I stood, but none touched the Pattern.

A mound of darkness half hidden from view began to extend blunt limbs in all directions. Grass withered as its black tendrils passed. Whole trees turned gray and fell to dust. The air grew cold, and my breath misted before me.

When I looked up, the sky boiled and seethed. Deep blue gave way to riots of black and yellow, all clotted up with stars that moved. It reminded me of the sky in the Courts of Chaos — but not quite the same.

I closed my eyes again, *feeling* the comfortably familiar lines of the Pattern around me. It radiated a power, a magical force that suffused me.

As I willed it so, the Pattern began to move. Up and up — larger — its lines beginning to turn like the spokes of a wheel. A wild and powerful joy filled me. *Yes!* Higher and faster — together — one being — we flew up into a boiling sky —

A cold darkness slammed down on me, a bone-crushing force that sent me reeling. I gasped with pain and shock. Spikes of fire went through my arms and legs and back. My mouth opened, and I heard myself beginning to scream.

Again it hit — then a third time — battering at me . . . pinning me down and crushing me.

And yet it could not kill me.

I drew into myself, gathering strength. All around me, shadows danced — a complex pattern of dark and light, like pieces of a giant puzzle now interlocked, now breaking apart — a mix of black and white blending to gray —

And through it all, dark tendrils *reached* —

"Yes!" I breathed.

I saw it now.

I *had* it.

Gathering myself, I whirled the Pattern like a shield, blocking, protecting. It couldn't get to me anymore. A howl sounded in my mind. Could it be . . . frustrated?

I felt myself rising up. The Pattern blazed now, a beacon in the darkness. The shadows leaped and gibbered and fled.

And still the shadow-creature struck. It came at me faster and harder this time, with a blast of cold that stung my face and chest. Distantly, as though in a dream, I felt a shudder run through my body . . . my *real* body, so far away it might have belonged to someone else.

I embraced the Pattern. The cold and the pain vanished. Another shudder ran through me . . . but pleasure this time, a joy greater than any I had felt before.

The Pattern would protect me.

Safe.

I wrapped it around my body like a protective cloak.

Together.

We joined.

We are one.

The universe spun around me, lights of stars, spaced with voids where strange intelligences moved and watched and played their games. Darkness flickered across their board. Pieces made of shadow and light hammered and clawed and poked and struck. None reached me in my cocoon. Weird voices screamed senseless threats, childish distractions, but I laughed as I would laugh at gnats in a summer garden. None of them mattered.

No. The darkness mattered.

I focused my complete attention on it. There — far below me — a tide of darkness rose around my physical body. I reached with my mind, covered my flesh with the Pattern, and watched the darkness wash harmlessly past.

My turn.

I could see it now . . . this odd, misshapen creature. Its whole enormous body extended through dozens of Shadows. Only one small part of it had reached the Pattern; the rest sat alone and far away like some grotesque toad waiting for a fly to pass.

As it probed at the Pattern, trying to get at my body, a vague sense of its frustration reached me. No matter what it did, no matter what it tried, it could not reach me.

Freda had been right. I *was* safe here.

But safety would not help the rest of my family, nor could it protect Amber. Whatever it took, I had to stop the creature. More than that, I had to destroy it utterly. It could never be allowed to leave this place alive.

How?

With my mind, with my thoughts, I held the Pattern. Now I took it and shaped it into a glowing sword. As the shadow-creature coiled about my body, I struck hard and deep.

A wordless, voiceless shriek sounded. The creature recoiled, pulling back.

Yes! I cried. I had hurt it. I could stop it.

Like a puppet-master, I pulled my body to its feet. Let my physical form be a distraction: the creature would attack my body . . . and while it did, I would strike.

I whirled my body around, facing the creature.

"I know you," I said to it, moving my jaws and tongue to form the words. "You are nothing here. Be gone!"

It flailed at me with blunt and useless limbs. But the Pattern around my body kept me safe.

I raised my body's hands, gathering strength into myself. All around me, the Pattern coiled with new life, its glow deepening. Light and power transfixed me.

I knew true strength for the first time in my life.

Now! I cried.

Together, we struck the shadow-creature. The Pattern blazed everywhere, so bright I could not see.

The shriek became a mindless scream.

Grimly, I reached out, pulling the Pattern *into* myself. Like a river of fire, it coursed through my body and soul.

I opened my eyes and saw through my physical body. At the same time, I saw the whole scene as though from a great height. In a thousand worlds, in a thousand ways, I reached out to grasp the shadow-creature, the whole of it, from one world to the next to the next. It writhed like a serpent, twisting over and over, plunging me headfirst into dark and light, heat and cold, night and day.

The universe reeled. And then it splintered.

I opened a thousand different eyes and stood on a thousand different worlds, all at the same time. As ash sifted from a leaden sky, shadow-faced men in leather armor and red-plumed helms pounded nails into my hands. "Fools," I told them. "This is but one of my infinite aspects." In another world, I sat in a temple with a giant pearl in my lap, while winged monkeys chewed the meat from my legs. In yet another, I stood on a hilltop while a warm rain burned my cheeks and eyes. In a valley below, the half-melted ruins of a once-mighty city glowed with a sickly green light. Twisted, burnt men and women with flesh peeling from their bones, their eyes a blind white, clawed their way toward me with outstretched hands, crying in pitiful voices, *"Heal us! Heal us!"*

And there were more — so many more that I could not take them in, each more horrible than the last.

And then . . .

A calmness settled over me. I saw, as through the mists of the ages, an Amber much changed. The castle had been expanded vastly so it covered three or four times as much area, with green and golden spires and sweeping terraces. And the city surrounding it! Thousands of buildings . . . a huge harbor crowded with ships . . . and all the people! Tens of thousands of men and women lived here now, in a bustling, thriving city greater than anything I had dared to imagine. The wide promenades decked with flowers of gold and red . . . palaces, temples, and more!

And in the center of the great audience hall . . . there on a throne of gold and jewels sat a burly man in his late middle age, broad of chest and strong of arm, dressed all in royal colors. On his head sat a jeweled crown, and at his side he kept a magnificent jeweled sword the likes of which I had never seen before.

The man on the throne was *me*. The weight of power showed in my old features, but I seemed happy, safe, and strong. And Amber had not only survived, but thrived.

Was this a vision of the future? A glimpse of what lay in store for Amber? Or just one possibility, which I would have to work to achieve?

I closed my eyes; the future vanished.

Distractions. Those visions did not matter now. I had to keep myself alive first.

For the first time, I brought the full force of the Pattern to bear on the shadow-creature. It — this *thing* — attacked on more than one level. Physically. Psychically. I would not allow any visions to distract me.

Bearing down with the Pattern, I heard it cry out.

PAIN — PAIN — PAIN —

I could hurt it. I had drawn first blood. Clearly the shadow-creature felt something when I attacked it with the Pattern.

The sense of pain came not with words, but as a *feeling* — a *sensation*. I knew it was not my own.

Whose? The shadow's?

. . . Or did it belong to someone else . . . someone controlling the creature? King Swayvil? Someone else from Chaos?

Still it reached for me.

DIE —

I heard it this time, as clear as a voice.

I cried, *"Get out of my head!"*

DIE — DIE — DIE —

Howling with rage, I raised the Pattern and struck again. *Keep out of my head! Out!*

It began to scream.

And, for the first time, I knew I would win. I focused all my attention on the creature and bore down upon it.

The Pattern began to unravel, loose threads of power flying all around me. The universe trembled. Stars began to rain down.

Still I pressed my attack, surrounding and tightening, going for a stranglehold — a death-grip. Distantly, something sizzled like flesh on fire. Then came strange sharp smells — acrid, metallic —

Noises that bled —

Sounds of fire and metal —

Colors I had never seen nor imagined —

HOW CAN YOU DO THIS THING?

The words boomed in my head. No, not words . . . *thoughts*. The shadow was not only alive, but intelligent. I could hear it clearly.

YOU ARE UNWORTHY.

I am the Pattern, I said to it, pulling the whole of the universe into myself. *Behold My power, and tremble at My wrath!*

The Pattern filled me now, so much fire and light and power that we blazed like the noontime sun.

I *was* the sun.

I *was* the fire.

I was all that, and far more!

Like a child with a plaything, I seized the creature . . . pulled it to me . . .

. . . and squeezed . . .

. . . and squeezed . . .

. . . and *squeezed* . . .

NO —

A gasping cry sounded.

PAIN —

Pain . . .

pain . . .

And suddenly I clutched at nothingness. Tatters of darkness flew up and away, dust motes caught in a cosmic maelstrom —

— vanishing —

Going . . .

going . . .

gone.

I opened my eyes. For the longest time I stared up into an infinite blue sky.

Was it . . . over?

It took a minute, but I finally remembered to breathe.

FIVE

lowly, groaning loudly, my voice like a rusty nail, I managed to roll over. It seemed to take an eternity and happen in slow motion, as if time had somehow paused while my mind raced far ahead. My entire body felt heavy . . . strange and numb . . . and somehow *wrong.*

Now, lying on my side, I managed to pry open my eyes. I thought I still lay at the center of the Pattern, but it was hard to tell. Colors blurred and ran; strange voices whispered at the edges of my perception, and though I strained to hear them, I could make no sense of any words — if those *were* words.

My whole body felt cold and sick. I knew my fight with that shadow-creature had taken place partly here and partly elsewhere, on some mental or spiritual plain I could not really comprehend. It came back in vague, disjointed flashes. There had been a joining of some kind. Had I really become one with the Pattern, or was my mind confused by whatever had taken place?

I shuddered softly. Then, taking a gulp of air, I forced myself into an upright sitting position. My body felt old and badly used. My muscles ached. My bones and joints creaked as though they hadn't been moved in months. My head throbbed fiercely.

First things first. Slowly, I took inventory of my body, inspecting hands, then wrists, then arms. All intact . . . not so much as a scratch. When I ran fingers over my face and gingerly probed my skull, I found no damage at all.

Apparently I had not been hurt physically. Yet I still felt *wrong*, somehow . . . deeply bruised and battered, as though I had been through the worst fight of my life.

I couldn't just sit here, though. Everyone in Amber must be wondering what had happened. I had to get back and let them know.

Gingerly, I climbed to my feet, swaying slightly. The stone slab seemed to tilt and slide underneath me. Still the colors bled; still the voices whispered.

Taking another deep breath, I pressed my eyes shut. I needed patience. Breathe — catch my wind — let my sense of balance return. I would recover from everything in time. The fight must have taken more out of me than I'd realized.

Slowly I leaned my head back, feeling the warmth of the sun on my face. Finally the whispers stopped. When at last I opened my eyes, I stared up into a dazzling, cloudless blue sky that stretched on and on. The colors had grown steady, too. I had just needed a few minutes to recover.

Slowly I turned, inspecting the trees around the edge of the stone slab. The Feynim creature had destroyed a large section of the forest, but already new saplings had sprouted amid the ruined, splintered stumps.

And as for the Pattern itself . . . I gaped in shock as the changes became apparent.

The Pattern had taken a lot of damage. Half of its lines had become twisted, somehow *distorted*. And, like the sands of an hourglass, those lines were now moving — drifting back to their former configurations.

Watching it made my head ache. Pressing fists to my eyes, I shut out the horrible vision and forced my attention away.

Some things should never be seen. The Pattern returning to its old shape and design stretched my mind in all the wrong ways, leaving me dizzy and disoriented.

I had to get away. I couldn't stay here while those changes were going on.

"Back to Amber," I said aloud. The Pattern had the ability to transport me anywhere I wanted to go once I reached its center. "Send me back to Amber. I want to go home!"

I willed it to happen, but nothing changed. I still stood in the middle of the Pattern, with its lines slowly drifting around me.

Perhaps it wasn't ready yet. If the Pattern didn't have the strength to send me through Shadows, I would have to let it finish . . . let it *heal*.

I sank down on my haunches to wait, amid the ever-shifting coils and folds and lines. Closing my eyes, I slowed my breathing and tried to rest as much as possible. I needed to recover as much as the Pattern did.

Idly, with my thumb, I gently rubbed the ring on my right index finger. The spikard gripped me loosely now; no new threats . . . I could relax for the moment. But how long until the next attack?

Time at the Pattern is a fairly meaningless thing. It could have been days or weeks or months; it could have been minutes. Neither hunger nor thirst bothered me. I felt no need to relieve myself. I listened to the restful silence, felt my heart thudding steadily in my chest, and waited as vast but unknowable forces worked around me.

After what seemed an eternity, my dizziness left like a receding tide. Opening my eyes, I rose unsteadily to my feet and looked around.

The Pattern looked as it always had . . . and yet, something bothered me. Some small, subtle detail I couldn't quite identify seemed wrong. *Different.*

Frowning, I turned slowly, studying the grand design. Yes, something had definitely changed. The lines had *shifted* in subtle ways, adding a slight new curve here, a slight tilt there, giving everything a fractionally new dimension. In places, some of the lines almost overlaid themselves.

It hadn't been this way before . . . had it? Somehow, I couldn't quite remember.

Everything *seemed* right again. As I turned, the full power of the Pattern filled me: strong and sure, flowing like an invisible river just beneath the surface of this place, vast and deep.

I looked beyond the Pattern. The last of the shattered trees had disappeared while I had slept, the splintered stumps and broken branches replaced by lush old-growth trees. Every single one looked as though it had been here since the dawn of time.

Slowly I nodded. All in all, a good job. Whatever the Pattern and I had done to defeat the creature, it had worked.

Perhaps Dad would be able to explain the changes. I would have to bring him back with me . . . assuming, of course, that the Pattern let me leave now.

Suddenly the ring on my finger pulsed sharply in warning. I jolted upright, scanning the treeline. Had the creature somehow survived? Or had another come to continue the attack?

Movement caught the corner of my eye. I whirled, one hand falling to the sword at my side.

A man in a shimmering gray tunic paced the outside edge of the Pattern, his gait odd but smooth. No, not a man — this fellow had extra joints in his legs. He had a bald, slightly elongated head, and grayish skin stretched tightly across his face . . . one of the Feynim.

"What are you doing here?" I called across to him.

The Feynim smiled faintly. He moved with a sinuous grace, never still, always circling, always watching me.

"Man. Oberon," he said. His ears twitched forward, almost like a horse's.

"Yes," I said. "I am Oberon."

"Strong. Alive are. Yet more."

More? What did he mean by that? I frowned.

"Yes," I said, though I didn't understand. The fey did not think like men; they seemed to have trouble translating concepts into words I could understand.

"Oberon," he said again, half nodding.

"What do you want?" I asked cautiously, still turning to follow his progress. He certainly seemed friendly enough. So why had my ring warned me about him?

"Come." He motioned me closer. In an insistent voice, he added, "Now return me."

I hesitated. Did he pose some threat? Hadn't Freda said the shadow-creature belonged to the Feynim . . . or at least to their world? Could the have sent the creature to destroy me — and might he now try to finish the job if I joined him?

Yet he didn't seem angry or threatening. He seemed, more than anything else, cautiously curious. Of course, that could be an act to throw me off-guard.

Even though the Pattern had the ability to send me anywhere I wanted to go — assuming it worked now — I couldn't wish myself away. For all I knew, this Feynim might be here to finish destroying the Pattern. Better to join him and keep an eye on his actions.

"Now return me," he said insistently.

"Return where?"

"Now home?" he said.

I willed myself next to him, and with a disconcerting rush, the Pattern moved me to his side. At least its powers seemed to have returned.

"Why are you here?" I demanded again, stepping forward and blocking his path.

He drew up short.

"Yes, here," he said. "Return now."

"Where? Amber?"

"Return . . . with . . ." He seemed to be struggling with the words. ". . . me?"

"All right," I said cautiously. "I'll use a Trump. I think Dad would like to meet you, anyway. We both have a lot of questions."

With one hand, I drew open the pouch at my belt and fumbled

inside for the Trump showing my father. With the other, I reached for the feynim's arm — but my fingers passed through his flesh and bone. I felt a cold dampness, like fog . . . as insubstantial as the creature I had just fought.

He must have felt my touch, though. He looked distinctly annoyed and took a hopping step back.

"No," he said. "No this."

"Then what do you want?" I demanded again. I advanced toward him, keeping our distance close. "Why are you here? Why did you send that creature after me? Tell me!"

He took another slight hop back, then seemed to fold into himself. I had seen that trick before, and I leaped to grab him — but found myself clutching empty air.

Gone.

I cursed. Not that I could have stopped him. My hand had already passed through him once . . . just like swords and knives had passed through the shadow-creature. It seemed to confirm Freda's theory that the Feynim had sent it after me.

But *why*? What had *I* ever done to them?

Frowning unhappily, I shook my head. Too many mysteries. Clearly I needed to find out more about the Feynim. They were up to something, and I didn't like it.

Grumbling half to myself, I pulled out my deck of Trumps and flipped through them until I came to one that showed a red-haired woman. Her dark eyes accentuated the paleness of her skin. Although her face had been drawn in simple lines, showing off the accents of her high cheekbones, a haughty, superior expression carried through. The artist — my brother Aber, long dead at my own hand for betraying me to the King of Chaos — had truly caught the essence of my sister Freda.

I raised the Trump and studied her face, concentrating on her image. In a heartbeat I felt an answering contact and gazed upon her face. She sat in a dark room before a table spread with Trumps. Reading the future again?

"Oberon!" she cried when she recognized me, smiling with honest pleasure. "We have all been worried — are you all right?"

"I'm fine. I destroyed the shadow-creature, but our battle left me stuck at the Pattern for a while. Things are back to normal now, so . . ." I shrugged.

"I know what you mean." She nodded slowly. "And I knew you would kill it. Here — come home and tell me everything that happened."

Rising, she stretched out her hand, and I took it. She pulled me into the library at Castle Amber. Although many of the room's built-in bookcases had yet to be filled, Dad and Freda had already begun rebuilding their libraries. They had brought in hundreds if not thousands of books and scrolls from countless Shadows. A pair of human skulls serving as bookends stared back at me with gaping eyes. I chuckled; nice touch, that.

"Any predictions?" I asked, nodding toward the table at the center of the room where Freda's Trumps lay spread in an intricate circular pattern. "I could use some good news right now. Long life and happiness, perhaps?"

"But you refuse to believe in fortune-telling."

I laughed. "It has its uses."

Several comfortable-looking chairs had been added to the décor since the last time I had been here, and I unbuckled my sword and settled gratefully into one. I must have been more tired than I thought; suddenly I wanted to curl up and go to sleep. But first I had to find out what — if anything — had happened in my absence.

I said, "Did I miss anything?"

"You will need a drink first. May I?"

Without waiting for my reply, she crossed to a small cart and filled a pair of matching crystal goblets from a cut-glass decanter.

I frowned. Something must be wrong. Then she brought both goblets over and handed one to me.

"Drink up, Oberon."

I raised mine in a silent toast, then sipped. Whiskey, nicely aged — just what I needed right now. It sent a nice burn down my throat and into my stomach.

"And?" I prompted.

"Tell me what happened to you, first," Freda said. "You said the creature is dead?"

"You were right about it," I said. Slowly I stretched out my legs. The alcohol had begun to warm me inside; I could have gone to sleep on the spot. "The Feynim sent it. I have no doubt about that."

"And you killed it?

"I used the Pattern, as you suggested."

"How?"

"I . . . I'm not sure. Everything got a little muddled toward the end."

She looked at me oddly. "Did anything else happen, Oberon?"

I did not mention my visions of other Shadows, or what might have been the future. She believed too much in prophecies and prediction; I didn't want to frighten her — or give her a false sense of security.

Instead, I said, "One of the Feynim showed up after the fight and tried to question me. It ran away when I touched its arm — my hand passed right through it, just like it passed through the creature."

"A sending . . ." She looked away, gaze distant.

I leaned forward. "A sending? What's that?"

"He sent an image of himself to talk with you, rather than go personally."

"Oh." That made sense. I distantly recalled something about the Feynim's creature existing on a different world and sending a small part of itself after me.

"Anyway," I continued, "when I demanded answers to my questions, he simply disappeared. Then I called you and came home."

"What else?"

"Isn't one epic battle across the Shadows with my life at stake enough?" I laughed.

"Nothing more? You are sure?" She stared at me in disbelief. "Oberon — you have been gone for more than three months!"

"What!" I shook my head in disbelief. Three months? Impossible! "It couldn't have been more than a day . . . maybe two at the most, with time running differently among the Shadows!"

"It *is* true." Her voice dropped, low and urgent. "We last spoke three months ago, when you led that creature off into Shadow."

I shifted uncomfortably, not liking the implications. It must have taken the Pattern a lot longer to fix itself than I had believed. The new trees *had* seemed to grow quickly. I must have slept through three months while I waited. No wonder Freda had given me a drink.

"Three months is a long time," I said. "What happened here? Did Swayvil attack Amber?"

"No, but we had all we could do to survive. A strange, magical storm came up — it lasted all the time you were gone, sometimes strong, sometimes weak, but always present. We suffered lightning but no rain, winds that tore up everything not nailed down, and a horrible pressure in the air. It gave everyone headaches for days at a time and set tempers on edge."

"Why didn't you go to another Shadow?"

"Conner and I tried. We could not use our Trumps, and when we moved between Shadows on our own, we found the same storm raging in all of them. We must have gone to fifty different worlds trying to escape."

"So you came back here?"

"Yes. It has been . . . difficult without you. Conner nearly strangled Father a dozen times."

I snorted. "I'd pay to see that. But this storm . . . could it have been an attack?" Swayvil had used storms against our family when we had gathered — so long ago it almost seemed a childhood dream! — in our father's keep in Juniper. Lightning blasted apart the stone walls and towers, killing many people.

"I do not believe it was an attack," she said. "No one directed these lightning strikes. Most hit iron rods on the tower roofs, doing little harm. The winds did most of the damage. Then everything cleared up a few hours ago." She waved toward the balcony. "You cannot see much now — but in the morning you will want to view the damage to Castle Amber. It will takes months to repair."

She made it sound so bad, I had to see for myself. Rising, I hurried to the balcony doors, threw them open, and strode outside. Broken clay roof-tiles crunched loudly under my boots. Scaffolding lay crumpled against the wall to the left where it had fallen from above.

With the storm gone, it seemed like a perfect night, the cloudless sky flecked with stars, a gentle breeze from the east, and a bright half-moon hanging over the sea. I picked my way around loose stones, roof-tiles, and broken wooden beams to the balcony railing. When I turned and looked up at the towers, a jagged black outline of what remained of the west tower stood silhouetted against the stars. Half the tower had collapsed. We were fortunate the whole castle hadn't fallen in. I would have to talk to the architects about making the supports stronger.

I sighed and turned my attention to the surrounding lands. From here I could see all the way to the sea, with its choppy waves that glistened with silver highlights. Many trees had fallen.

Freda joined me, and I heard a faint sob escape from her. She was neither as strong nor as ruthless as she liked to pretend. Wordlessly, I put my arm around her shoulder and pulled her close.

"Oberon . . ." she whispered.

"The worst is over," I said with more conviction than I felt. "The Feynim know I can destroy their creatures. They will not send another one."

"I hope you are right."

I continued to look across the castle. The east tower had lost its roof, and everywhere large patches of thatching or shingles had been ripped away by the wind. As Freda said, it would take months to get the castle put right again.

"Was anyone hurt?" I asked.

"Not severely. Almost everyone took shelter in the grand ballroom when the storm grew bad."

"Good." Thank the gods we hadn't lost anyone. "Almost everyone?" I asked.

"Father refused to leave his workshop."

I smiled thinly. "Probably working on a solution to the storm. What about the soldiers?" A force of more than one hundred and fifty thousand fighting men had been camped to the north when I left — drilling and training to protect the castle from King Swayvil and the armies of Chaos.

"They suffered some casualties, I believe. Conner will be able to tell you when he returns."

"He's not here?"

She pulled away. "He took a scouting party out as soon as the storm broke. He feared an attack from Chaos might be coming."

I nodded; that had been a good idea. I'd let him finish rather than call him back with a Trump, just in case. It never hurt to be paranoid where King Swayvil and the Courts of Chaos were concerned.

Sudden light and motion in the courtyard below caught my eye. I leaned over the railing and peered down.

Using torches, workers had already begun their cleanup, hauling away débris in small carts and barrows. They looked tired and worn, and not from their work. The storm must have taken its toll on everyone here.

I'd have to do something to raise my people's spirits. Perhaps a holiday in honor of my return? "King Oberon Day" or "Victory Day" or some such . . .

Behind us, I heard the door to the library open. My ring had not warned me, but one hand reached instinctively for the hilt of my sword — which wasn't there. I had taken it off inside.

Fortunately, it was only a servant in castle livery. He carried a large tray heavily laden with dishes, bowls, and baskets. Food? I sniffed hungrily.

The man carefully lowered his tray onto the table next to my sword, turned and bowed to us both, then left without a word. He had the good sense to pull the door shut behind himself.

"You have them well trained," I said, heading inside. "I'm starving, and I didn't even realize it!"

"I ordered a late supper before you got here," Freda said, heading back inside. "You look as though you need it more than I do, however."

"I'm sure there's enough for two."

Reaching the tray, I began lifting lids to investigate. Everything smelled delicious. Cold salted meats . . . several warm spiced vegetable dishes . . . sliced red apples . . . a loaf of warm, crusty brown bread . . . a nice selection of finger-cakes and pastries . . . and most welcome of all, a large pitcher of mulled red wine. The tray even included place settings for four. We wouldn't have to share a plate or silverware.

As I poured wine for both of us, Freda gathered up her Trumps and put them away in a little silver box. Then she wiped her hands on a napkin and began serving us both generous portions of meat and vegetables. My mouth started to water and my stomach rumbled; if three months had passed, suddenly I felt it.

"You never told me what you saw in your cards," I said as she passed me my plate.

"Besides the storm —" she began.

I had just raised my fork to take my first bite when the door burst open. Cursing madly, our father stormed in. He was a short, dwarfish man with a slight twist to his lips that gave him either a sinister or comical appearance depending on the way he tilted his head. Right now, in the lamplight, he looked positively fiendish.

"There you are!" he cried. "I knew you had returned, my boy! Are you done fooling around with the Pattern? You're going to wreck everything if you keep it up!"

I had no idea what he was talking about, so I ignored him and took my bite of salted beef. Despite being too cold, too salty, and far too chewy, it ranked among the most delicious foods I had ever tasted.

"Oberon!" he snapped, hands on his hips, glaring. "Are you deaf? You have to come with me, and *right now*!"

"I'm eating."

"But the Pattern —!"

"Is it important?" I asked. Poking a slice of apple with my fork, I popped it into my mouth and chewed slowly, not looking at him.

"Important? *Important?*" he shouted. "You're going to destroy *everything*!"

I threw down my fork in disgust. Clearly he had no intention of letting me eat in peace.

"What in the seven hells are you talking about, Dad?" I demanded. "What have I done this time?"

"The Pattern!" he howled. "You moved it here! *It's inside the castle!*"

"What!" I leaped to my feet. How could that be? The Pattern couldn't be moved — it had been etched into solid stone!

"You heard me!" he said. "How did you do it? And can you put it back? It cannot possibly stay here — it will not be safe!"

"Wait, wait!" I held up my hand and his voice trailed off. "Where is it? Show it to me!"

"Come on, come on, quickly now!" Turning, he darted into the hall. He was muttering things under his breath about "stupid tricks" and "fool children."

Freda's eyes met mine, and I saw deep concern mixed with puzzlement. She didn't know anything about the movement of the Pattern.

"Come on, we must see what he is talking about," she said, rising. "It sounds serious."

"Right." I paused long enough to grab my sword and a handful of apple slices. Clearly, this wasn't my day.

SIX

arrying oil lanterns, Dad and I descended flight after flight of stairs, heading into the lowest levels of the castle. Freda walked between us. I kept glancing left and right as we walked, surprised at the progress made over the last three months. Workmen had carved out chambers for use as storerooms, wine cellars, and dungeon cells, per the master blueprints drawn up by our architects. With the storm raging outside, they must have concentrated their efforts down here.

The air grew damp and chill; we passed through several low-ceilinged rooms and emerged into a cavernous chamber that wasn't on any blueprint I had ever approved. An eerie blue light shimmered from a long inward-circling line traced into the stone floor. Of course, I recognized it at once — it had the right size and the right shape down to every line and curve: it *was* the Pattern.

No wonder Dad thought I had moved it here. It looked exactly like the one I had just left behind.

How was this possible? How could it exist in two places at the same time? Had someone made a secret copy when we weren't looking?

That couldn't be the answer. Nobody could have copied it here, or anywhere else for that matter. Dad had drawn the original Pattern using his own blood. I couldn't think of anyone other than the two of us who knew the Pattern well enough to do that.

"How did you move it here?" he demanded again, waving angrily at the floor. "Do you know how many problems you will cause?"

"I . . . didn't do it." As I walked closer, studying its lines, my skin started to prickle all over. A deep power radiated from this Pattern, too, a tangible force that resonated deep inside me.

"Are you sure this is the *real* Pattern?" Freda asked slowly. "It looks right, but . . ."

"Feel its power!" Dad said. I knew what he meant. Up close, it fairly rippled with currents of energy. "This *is* the Pattern. No one can mistake it."

"Unfortunately," I said, "you're wrong. I left the original Pattern — the one you made — a few minutes ago, Dad. It hasn't been moved. Somehow, it's been copied."

"Impossible!" he snapped.

"Let's find out," I said. "Hold my lantern."

When he took it, I drew out my set of Trumps and leafed through it. Finally I found the one which showed the original Pattern surrounded by its silent forest of trees.

I studied it, and the image came to life before me. Grabbing my father's arm, I stepped forward, dragging him along.

It was still day at the original Pattern — it always seemed to be day when I visited here — and as we stood before that immense slab of stone traced with the winding blue line that made the original Pattern, I felt waves of energy coming from its surface. It seemed exactly like the one we had just left in Amber. I could see no differences anywhere, no matter how hard I looked.

"How is this possible?" Dad mumbled to himself. He began to circle the slab, studying the Pattern's lines.

"I don't know," I admitted. I hurried to catch up. "If you didn't make the one in the castle, and I know *I* didn't . . . who else has that power?"

"No one!"

"King Swayvil?" It seemed unlikely. But the King of Chaos had access to magics I could barely comprehend.

"He would destroy the Pattern, not create a second one."

"Maybe he's planning something . . ."

"He is not to blame this time. We must find another answer."

Dad turned slowly, studying the trees around us as though looking for something . . . or someone. The unicorn? She had led me here before. She had been present when Dad came here originally. In fact, she seemed to appear whenever anything happened involving the Pattern.

Yet she did not appear this time.

"She's not coming," I finally said.

"I guess not." He glanced at me, then started around the Pattern once more. "You must have done *something* to bring it into existence. Think, boy!"

There had been my fight with the Feynim's creature. I had used the Pattern to defend myself. Could something have happened then?

A horrible realization suddenly came to me. Maybe I *had* done it.

"At one point," I said, "when I was here with the Feynim's creature, the universe seemed to shatter — but it came back together again, including the Pattern."

"It *shattered*?" he frowned, brow wrinkling. "What does *that* mean? Tell me *exactly* what happened — *exactly* what you did!"

"*Shattered.*" I shrugged helplessly. "I don't know how else to describe it. Somehow, I became part of the Pattern. We were a single being . . . or at least, that's how it felt. Something happened when the Feynim's creature attacked me. Everything seemed to break apart, and I found myself in many different Shadows at once, each more horrible than the last. My memory is still pretty fuzzy. It was more than I could take in at once."

We finished our circumnavigation of the Pattern, and Dad began muttering softly to himself. He started around it a second time. Still I followed.

"Well?" I prompted. "What happened? Do you know?"

"A better question," he said, "might be — is the Pattern in Amber the only copy?"

I stared at him, horrorstruck. "There may be *more*? Where? How many?"

"Anywhere! Everywhere! There could be one in every single Shadow, for all I know. Or there may be none at all." He frowned. "Your longtime presence in Amber — so close to the Pattern and the source of your power — may have brought it there. Who can say? Not I! Not now! Not yet!"

"But you think it's possible?" I pressed. "You think there might be more than one copy?"

"We must face that possibility."

"Maybe it's a good thing," I mused. "If every world has its own

Pattern, Swayvil would never be able to destroy them all. It might make us safer."

"Or," he said, "you would never be able to guard them all. Perhaps, if he destroys one, he will be destroying them all — for they are all aspects of a single creation!"

I felt the blood drain from my face. That would make us more vulnerable than every before. We would never be able to defend every Pattern on every Shadow.

"Let us hope," he said darkly, "that only one copy now exists. More than that would be a disaster."

I felt a flicker of contact at the back of my mind.

"Wait," I said. "Someone is trying to reach me wtih a Trump."

I focused my attention on the contact. A second later, I saw Freda before me. She still stood in the underground chamber; I could see the blue glow of the Pattern behind her.

"Oberon?" she asked. "Are you all right? Do you want to come back?"

"Yes," I said. We couldn't do much more here. Best to return to Amber.

Freda stretched out her hand to me. I took it, again dragging Dad along. Then we all stood together in the underground room with the Amber-Pattern again. This time, though, the chamber shone with a brilliant white light — three dazzling globes floating in mid-air, just above Freda's head.

"Where did those come from?" I said, staring up at them.

"I made them," Freda said. She sounded more than a little annoyed. "You left with the lanterns, after all. I hate it down here, and I find my own lights comforting."

"Sorry," I said.

"Mph." She still looked annoyed. "Take more care next time. I would have liked to have seen the original Pattern, too. I have never been there."

"Next time." I turned to our father. "At least *our* copy of the Pattern is underground," I said. "We can seal off this room easily enough and place guards over it. Anyone who wants to destroy it will have to take the castle first."

Dad nodded slowly. "A good idea. There is no reason for anyone but you or me to come in here. And, of course, it would probably kill anyone but you who tried to walk it. It is attuned to you . . . and you alone."

"Let us talk about it in the library," Freda said. Her voice sounded tired. Perhaps nearness to the Pattern had begun to affect her. "I hate being down here."

"Go ahead," I told her gently. "We will join you in a minute. We still have a few things to discuss first."

Nodding, she headed back the way we had come. All three balls of light bobbed along in her wake, leaving Dad and me with just our lanterns and the bluish glow of the Pattern for illumination.

"How did you find this copy?" I asked him. We would have to find a name for it. The Amber-Pattern?

"Workmen assessing damage to the castle foundations stumbled across it half an hour ago. One of them stepped on it." He pointed to a faint grayish smudge at the edge of the Pattern. "As you can see, it destroyed him — 'burned him up' — his partner said."

"The Pattern did *that*?" I asked in surprise. "Surely he wasn't a threat —"

"The Pattern defends itself . . . much as the Logrus does against those not born of Chaos."

I nodded; it made sense to me.

"Did you noticed the changes in the Pattern?" I asked, pointing. "See — that part of the line has moved. And over there —"

"Yes." His eyes narrowed slightly, studying the glowing blue line. "It has been redrawn. And yet . . . if anything, it has become more perfect. Now it matches *exactly* what is within you."

"What do you mean, *exactly*?" I asked. "Didn't it match before?"

"Yes — mostly. I drew it, but I am a man born of Chaos, remember. I could not do the job perfectly no matter how hard I tried." He shrugged half apologetically. "I could always see a few slight imperfections where the line varied from its true course. An inch off here — a foot off there. It adds up. And yet it did not matter; it was close enough, and the Pattern functioned the way it was meant to."

"And now?"

He smiled slowly. "Now all my little errors have been fixed. Whoever copied the Pattern also corrected it — corrected them both. Was that you, my boy?"

I shook my head. "My fight with the Feynim-creature distorted the first Pattern. I used the Pattern to kill it — I'm still not quite sure how — but it left the Pattern tangled-up and misshapen. I had to sit and wait while it recovered its original form afterwards."

"You actually saw this happen?"

"Yes." I shuddered, remembering. "It was horrible!"

"Go on. Tell me what happened. Leave nothing out; it may prove important."

"Well . . . there isn't much to say. The line moved on its own, but slowly. I couldn't bear to watch, so I shut my eyes to wait it out. When I opened them again, everything had returned to normal. Even the trees surrounding the Pattern had grown back."

"This is good news. Very good news." He chortled happily to himself. "The Pattern is stronger than I had dared to hope. *It healed itself!* As long as its line remains unbroken, it will endure."

"The storm," I murmured, half to myself. "It took place while the Pattern healed. That's why it affected all of the Shadows Conner and Freda visited."

"Yes, yes, my boy! Exactly! You see it too — cause and effect; the two events are really the same!"

"Three months . . ." I swallowed. I couldn't believe I had slept that long. The Pattern must have been very badly hurt.

I asked, "Could the Feynim's creature have destroyed the Pattern? Was it strong enough to do that?"

"I doubt it. Not if the Pattern is as powerful as I suspect. But it could have done a great deal of damage had it injured *you*. Your blood — perhaps the blood of anyone in our family — may be strong enough to etch new lines, damaging or distorting the Pattern permanently."

"I was lucky, then." I would have to be more careful about bringing visitors to the true Pattern. If a bloody nose had the power to destroy our universe, I didn't want to take any chances.

Then I smiled. We might turn the new Pattern to our advantage.

"If the real Pattern is so vulnerable," I said, "let's forget about it."

"What do you mean?"

"Let's let everyone think *this* is the real Pattern. We'll guard it. We'll protect it with our lives. In years to come, when everyone knows about this Pattern, the true Pattern will be forgotten. And that will keep it safe."

"Yes . . ." he breathed. "Brilliant, my boy. Brilliant!"

I nodded. One less thing for me to worry about. I would have to hide or destroy my Trump of the true Pattern.

"If you don't mind," I said, "I'll leave you to post the guards. I still have a few things to discuss with Freda."

He waved me off. "Go ahead, my boy. Leave the Pattern to me. Your future is far more important."

"Future?" I said, puzzled. "What are you talking about?"

He threw back his head and howled with such laughter that I didn't know whether to take him seriously or not.

SEVEN

y father had been a little crazy since he drew the Pattern. I knew and accepted that fact, so I did not take his bizarre talk terribly seriously.

Right now, safety for Amber had to be my sole concern. If the Feynim had for some reason declared war upon us, we would have to be vigilant.

An elderly retainer intercepted me at the head of the stairs, requesting — quite politely and quite properly — my assistance with a domestic dispute in the kitchens. It seemed two of the skullery maids were at each other's throats . . . and the affections of one of the castle guards lay in the balance.

By the time I had settled everyone down and solved the problem (by threatening to roast the guard in question if he didn't pick one girlfriend and stick faithfully by her), half an hour had passed. Word seemed to be spreading rapidly about my return. Everywhere I went, I found grinning guards and servants eager to bow or salute and wish me a pleasant evening. They seemed in high spirits, despite three months of devastating winds and lightning.

And why not? The moment I had returned, the storm went away. They must have seen it as a sign of my power.

And by this time the architects had shown up to demand my

immediate attention. At their request, I took a whirlwind tour of the castle, listening to a long, dry lecture on the structural problems inherent in modern castle architecture.

I got the gist of it: the wind-damage, although considerable, was largely cosmetic. Lack of rain had a lot to do with it; although every roof had been damaged to some extent, no water had gotten inside to destroy the plaster, floorboards, or support beams.

By the time I freed myself from their vast array of questions and seemingly endless supply of blueprints and made it to the library, Freda had long since finished her meal, packed up her Trumps, and disappeared – undoubtedly gone to bed for the night. I couldn't blame her for that; fortunately, I could talk to her in the morning.

I stifled a yawn. Might as well return to my own room and catch up on some much-needed sleep. You never would have guessed I'd just had a three-month nap.

When I walked into my private chambers, I found no fewer than eight people hard at work. The glass panes in all the windows had blown in, and three sleepy-looking carpenters were hard at work replacing the last of them. My valet had just finished changed my bed's linens. Two maids with brooms and dustpans swept up blown-in dirt, broken bits of roof-tile, and shards of glass from the windows as two burly workmen untied and unrolled fresh carpets for the floor.

My valet hurried over. "Welcome home, Sire!" he cried, bowing.

"Thanks, Shaye," I said. I noticed that he had already taken the time to lay out my nightclothes on the bed, fluff up the feather pillows, and bring in fresh water for the washstand. "You're on top of everything as usual, I see."

"I do my best, Sire. Is there anything else you need?"

Peace with Chaos and the Feynim? King Swayvil's head on a silver platter?

I said, "No, I'm fine."

Then I shooed everyone out — acknowledging all the bowing with a few brief words of praise for such thoughtfulness and quick action above the call of duty. Finally, alone at last, I stripped, crawled into my bed, and almost instantly fell asleep.

Years ago, when King Swayvil had been stalking and murdering my family, I used to have prophetic dreams. Night after night I saw people I could not possible know and places I had never seen.

Tonight I felt another such dream coming on. A slight sense of disconnect washed over me, and I *knew* things were going to get strange in this vision. . . .

I am leaving Castle Amber and riding down to the sea on a black horse. The trees are in flower and a rain of yellow petals falls as I pass.

By the time I reach the water, it is night. A full, bright moon rides the heavens, and by its glow I see as clearly as day.

Past the windswept dunes and down to the water's edge I go. I do not stop, but ride straight for the water. My horse, Apollo, slows to a walk as low waves break across his hooves.

We wade out from the land. Water rises to my calves, spills over the tops of my boots, then reaches my waist. For a second my horse fights for his head, trying to turn back, but I steer him straight on. I am master here, and he will obey without question. We both know it.

Reluctantly he walks on, deeper, to his neck, to his muzzle. As the waves close over his head, still he walks on. Then it is my turn and the water closes over me.

I am soaking wet. I am chilled to the bone. My hair begins to float freely around my head.

More urgently, my lungs feel like they're on fire. Finally I can stand it no longer. I have to breathe in or my chest will burst.

Desperate now, I open my mouth and inhale – but somehow, impossibly, my lungs fill with something as sweet as air instead of sea-water.

Apollo continues his slow, plodding descent. Carefully he picks his way down an immense marble staircase. Statues to either side show web-handed men and women in various menacing poses. Some hold tridents; others hold swords. Their faces, drawn long and stern, gaze down at me as though considering some intricately planned doom.

The farther we go, the darker the water comes. Blue and murky, filled with tiny bubbles, it is hard to see through. I can only see a few yards ahead.

Yet, as we descend, I sense a lightening in the water before us, almost as though we are drawing nearer to something large and bright.

Sure enough, glowing spheres of light begin to appear between statues twenty feet farther ahead. They provide just enough illumination for us to see our way.

Apollo begins to stumble on the steps. He isn't built for traveling this way. I dismount, my movements vague and sluggish in the water. I will need time to get used to moving down here, but I know I can make better time on foot than riding.

When I give him his head, Apollo turns at once and gallops toward the surface as fast as he can. His movements are almost comical in the water, legs churning too fast, nostrils flared, eyes rolling wildly.

On foot now, I continue my descent. Cautiously I study each new statue as I pass. On some, the eyes seem to move, following my progress. Others simply glower. And the farther down I go, the more menacing each new figure becomes.

Finally, as buildings come into sight, a rising awe sweeps through me. These sprawling underwater houses, temples to unknown gods, and odd three-sided towers seem nothing short of incredible. My gaze drifts to a huge central complex with gold-capped domes and high turrets. Columns with intricate floral caps hold up all the roofs inside. A palace?

The architecture is magnificent. I continue to marvel at it as I continue my descent. Now I can see the end of the staircase . . . a huge stone gate in the shape of a dragon. And here, standing before the gate, I see people for the first time . . . two bare-chested men standing at attention. Both hold long-handled tridents in upright positions. Both have thick black hair with green highlights, now billowing in the water. As I near them, I note their green-hued lips, their deep green eyes flecked with gold. Even their nipples are dark green.

Though they stand as still as the statues I already passed, their eyes track my progress. And I can see their chests moving as they breathe.

Up close, I see webbing between their fingers as they grip their tridents. It must be hard to hold them that way, but they manage without complaint.

"I am King Oberon," I announce when I finally reach them. Somehow, I know they understand me. "I have been summoned."

Behind them, on the other side of the dragon gate, runs a street paved in blocks of some greenish-brown stone. Buildings to either side have tall, narrow windows through which dim faces peer down at me.

"The queen is expecting you," says one of the guards. His voice is like an ancient, rusted hinge. "Come with me."

Turning, he leads the way through street after street, heading toward a huge complex of buildings in the center of the city. Men, women, and children scatter as we approach, taking refuge inside the houses and shops. They all seem terrified of me. I feel the weight of hundreds of eyes staring down at us as we pass.

The magnificent complex of buildings at the center of the city is a palace. The closer we get to it, the more magnificent it appears. The golden domes, lofty spires, and arching walkways are like nothing I have ever seen before. Guards with tridents stand by every entrance, and more men with tridents patrol the upper walkways.

Through the main courtyard, up a broad flight of steps, and into a wide corridor we proceed. We pass more guards, and a squad of men with tridents marches by us. Servants bustling up and down are dressed in green silks. Like everyone else I have seen, their hair has green highlights. Bowing, they move aside for us.

At last we reach a large audience hall. Another dozen guards with tridents stand around a high throne that looks as if it's made of solid gold, and on that throne sits a woman of middling years. She must be their ruler. She is dressed in a long, dark green robe with pearls and small polished seashells embroidered on the hem and sleeves. More shells adorn a necklace and matching bracelets. On her head is a thin gold crown worked with the designs of shells and tridents.

As the guards march me up to her throne, the woman regards me with a haughty smile, looking down her long nose. Her eyes, as green as the depths of the ocean, look through me — and seemingly come up wanting.

I bow to her because it is expected.

"You are King Oberon." Her voice, low and fluid, falls like honey on my ears.

"I am. You must be Queen Moins."

"Yes."

"Why am I here?" I ask.

She rises. "You must undo that which you have wrought."

I tilt my head, puzzled. "I don't understand."

"Remove it! Remove the Pattern!"

"What Pattern?"

"Do you claim to know nothing of it?"

"Yes." I nod slowly. "I have no idea what you're talking about!"

She claps her hands. Underwater, the sound is muted rather than sharp, but her guards seem to understand it all too well. They lower their tridents and point them at my chest, surrounding me. I feel needle-sharp points digging into the small of my back, pricking my skin through the cloth of my shirt.

"What is it you want of me?" I ask.

"Get rid of him!" Queen Moins says, voice hard and cold. "The next time he comes, perhaps he will cooperate!"

The guards march me out of the throne room, back down the corridor, and out into a different courtyard. This one has what looks like a round wading fish-pond built of stone in the center, but I know it can't be filled with water or fish since we're already under the sea. As we draw near, I see a black swirling liquid inside. It moves slowly, a miniature and not very powerful whirlpool. Somehow, I sense it is a door.

"Get in!" says the man holding a pike at my back. "Jump!"

"Where does it lead?" I ask. I have no intention of going into the whirlpool. It might lead anywhere.

As he begins to answer, I turn suddenly, my right hand a blur as I go for the closest trident. My left hand grasps it and yanks it forward and to one side, *so it passes harmlessly beside my body. I sense all the guards surging forward at once, but the sea-water slows their movements.*

One hand punches the nearest guard in the nose, and after a sickening crunch, he falls back, trailing a stream of blood that rapidly clouds the water. My second blow hits another guard's throat, and he too is out of the fight, gasping and struggling to breathe.

The trident I hold is loose now. I grab it, spin, and run the nearest guard through the shoulder as he lunges toward me. He misses. Bracing my feet, I throw him up and over my head. He leaves a stream of blood and bubbles in the water. I let go, and he sails away, taking the trident with him.

I snatch up a fallen trident before the next two guards are on top of me. There is no hesitation in their attack. They separate, trying to divide my attention, jabbing at me.

I grip my weapon with my right hand. It's unwieldy here, underwater, and I'm moving far more slowly than I like. But I catch the tip of one trident against mine, thrust it aside, and go for a stranglehold with my left hand. I seize him, crush his throat, and throw him at the onrushing guards.

The last one is almost on top of me. I whirl again. He falls back before the slash of my trident — but instead of following through with the swing, I release its handle. It sails faster than a crossbow bolt and catches him in the chest, running him through. His dark blood jets into the water, a billowing cloud.

Off balance, I'm spinning backwards. My heel hits the edge of the pool and I topple into it, arms windmilling. There is no splash, but blackness wraps me as I fall —

    fall —

      fall —

    *   *   *

Gasping, I sat up. For a second, I didn't know where I was. Darkness —
cold — wet —

Bed.

Safe.

That too-real dream came back to me. Sweat must have soaked my
clothes and sheets. No wonder I had dreamed of being underwater. I
had never suffered from night-sweats before, and I hoped I wasn't
coming down with some sickness. Pneumonia?

When I sat up, though, the mattress made soft squishing sounds.
It seemed to be completely soaked. How much could one man sweat?

And why did it smell of sea-brine?

Carefully I licked my fingers, then spat to one side. *Salt water.* I really *had* been in the sea.

But how? What kind of dream took me into the water that way?
I have thought dreams could be made real, but enough impossible
things had happened in the last few years for me to wonder.

I fought to recall the details. Something about a palace under the
waves, ruled by a woman . . . and the Pattern had also been there . . .

Queen Moins, that was her name. Yes. It came back to me now. I
would have to ask Dad if he had ever heard of her before. Perhaps I
ought to try to contact her — that must be what my dream meant. But
what about the Pattern? She had wanted me to do something . . . get
rid of it? Could she also have a copy of it in her kingdom?

Rising, I wrapped myself in a blanket and wandered out onto the
balcony. Dawn had just broken, painting the east with fingers of pink
and yellow. Gray smudges of smoke rose from the kitchen chimneys.

As I gazed across my kingdom, I spotted two columns of men in the distance — perhaps fifty of them in all — with a dozen covered carriages following behind. They were clearly heading toward the castle.

Our first royal visitors! From some nearby, as-yet-undiscovered kingdom, perhaps?

I leaned forward, straining to see. The standard-bearer, as if in response, turned slightly, and I saw his banner clearly.

A coiled snake . . . they were from the Courts of Chaos.

EIGHT

orns began to blare from the guard-towers. Shouts echoed through the castle. Troops scrambled from the barracks, weapons in hand, and manned the walls.

At least they weren't sleeping on the job. While they mustered out, I ran back into my bedroom, dropping my blanket and throwing on clothes. Quickly, I buckled on my swordbelt, added a couple of knives, and laced up my boots. Lastly I brushed back my hair — finding a small piece of seaweed behind my right ear! — and placed a thin circlet of gold on my head. Today they would find a king in residence and ready to lead his troops into battle, if necessary.

And yet it occurred to me that this was a curiously small force for King Swayvil to send against us. Only fifty men, when I had fielded a million against him only three years ago? And what of those carriages?

All things considered, this couldn't possibly be an attack. Ambassadors might well be inside those carriages . . . along with gifts, apologies, and a suit for peace, perhaps?

I snorted. Not at all likely! Swayvil must have a more devious plan in mind. We would have to be on our guard.

By the time I reached the courtyard, I found the walls fully manned with archers, and a squad of pikemen stood ready to my left.

But the gates still yawned open, and no one seemed in a hurry to close them.

"Get up!" I bellowed, stalking forward. "Ready defenders!"

"Wait!" Freda called. She stood just inside the gates, talking to Captain Yoon.

Frowning, I jogged to her side. "What's the meaning of this?" I demanded.

"You had a chance to bathe," she said. "Good. We must look our best today."

Bathe? The seawater must have washed some of the grime off.

"Look our best for what?" I snapped. "Do you think I care how I look in the middle of a battle?"

"There will be no battle. And you must look good for Lord Dire's visit."

I stared blankly. "Lord Dire? Who is that?"

She sighed. "Oberon . . . I did not get a chance to tell you last night. I invited the Dires to visit us some time ago. We must not cut ourselves off from Chaos, after all —"

"Yes, we must!" I said sharply. "I want nothing to do with anyone from Chaos! They are nothing but trouble for me . . . for us all!"

"Lord Dire is powerful and influential. If he accepts us as equals, others in Chaos will, too . . . perhaps even King Swayvil himself, in time. Besides, I know you will like him. He too is a military man, and you will find you have much in common."

A visit . . . damnable timing. Why now, when I hadn't even had a chance to catch my breath?

Frowning, I glanced at the open gates. I couldn't do anything about it now without insulting this Lord Dire. And there was no sense in that, especially if he proved as sympathetic as Freda claimed.

"Very well," I said slowly. "But if this turns out to be a trick of some kind, I'll hang his head over the gates as an example to every other spy and murderer from the Courts of Chaos!"

"The Dires will not be any bother at all. Ask Father if you wish — he knows them quite well."

"I will!" I promised.

At the sound of hooves on stone, I turned. Dire's men had been on foot, of course, so it couldn't be them.

"Oberon!" my brother Conner shouted as he galloped into sight. He rode a large bay gelding, now wild-eyes and foam-flecked from a long, hard ride. He pulled up short and leaped from the saddle. "Men from Chaos —"

"I know," I said. "Freda invited them."

"What?" He stared across at her, but she only smiled sweetly.

I took his arm and drew him aside as a stableboy made off with his horse.

"Did you know anything about this visit from Lord Dire?" I asked quietly.

"It's Lord Dire?" He looked baffled. "Why would he visit *us*?"

"That's what I've been asking. Apparently Freda invited him and his wife. Do you know them?"

"Mostly by reputation. Lord Dire is said to be very ambitious . . . he wanted to be king of Chaos, I think, but never managed to gain enough support to seize power from King Uthor. I once tried to court his second daughter, Koé, but she ended up marrying Duke Harn, I believe. Her loss."

"They sound fairly harmless," I said. "As people from the Courts of Chaos go, anyway."

He shrugged. "Pretty much. Lord Dire hasn't been in favor in the Courts in many years. Dad knows him socially, of course, and Freda knows the whole family quite well — their third daughter, Della, is her best friend."

"Ah." Now things began to make sense. No wonder she wanted them here. "I bet Freda got lonely and invited them for company."

"I suppose." His frown deepened.

"Can you think of another reason?"

"Freda always has at least six reasons for everything she does. Her schemes are complex and far-reaching, and usually not so obvious as this one."

I chuckled and shook my head. Just what I needed — more family plots and politics. Besides, if she wanted company, I saw no great harm in it. As long as they minded their manners . . .

"I can always kick Lord Dire out," I said, "if he's come to cause trouble."

"Keep in mind that he's a longtime friend of our family. Don't insult him without cause. You may need him someday."

He sounded like Freda, but it still seemed like good advice. I nodded slowly.

"What about your scouting trip?" I asked. "Anything to report? Invaders? Cattle rustlers?"

He sighed and shook his head. "It went well enough, I suppose, from a tactical point of view. No forces are massing at our borders, preparing to attack and slaughter us. No one is at our borders at all . . . or anywhere else, for that matter. This still appears to be an empty Shadow. The biggest problem is all the wind-damage."

"It's not just around the castle?"

He shook his head. "It's everywhere. Whole sections of the forest have been flattened. It will take years for everything to return to normal — if it ever does."

About as I had expected; I nodded.

"What about your men?" I asked.

"We did some hunting while we were out. They're carrying three deer for the kitchens. At least we'll have fresh meat for the next few days."

"That's good news."

I glanced at Freda. She had wandered closer to the gate and had an eager, expectant look on her face. I had never seen her this excited before.

"Keep an eye on things here?" I said.

"Sure. Why?"

"I want to know everything that happens with Lord Dire when he arrives. I need to see Dad right now. I want to do a little checking on Lord Dire."

"All right. I'll give you a full report later."

Turning, I hurried back inside and soon tracked my father down in the library. He had been reading several old scrolls with a confused look on his face.

"Find anything interesting?" I asked, joining him.

"Not yet." He let the scroll roll back up and tucked it into a tube.

Carefully, he returned it to a shelf. "I posted guards over the Pattern," he continued. "The architects are down there now, evaluating the room. They have two entrances to close off."

"Good. Any idea what brought it here?"

"Not yet. But I will!"

I nodded. "There's something else I want to ask you. Have you ever heard of Lord Dire?"

"Dire? Of course! Nice old fellow, a good friend in olden days . . . to all of us. Why?"

"He's here."

"What!" He looked honestly surprised.

"Freda didn't tell you, either?"

"No." His brow creased. "Odd, that she would ask him without letting me know."

I thought so, too.

"Conner thinks she was lonely and wanted friends."

"Is the Dire girl . . . what is her name? Dell . . . Della? Yes, Della. A charming girl, going to be a real beauty someday. Is she here, too?"

"I don't know."

"Find out. She and Freda are the best of friends. If Della is here, it is because Freda wanted her."

I nodded slowly. "I wanted to ask you about something else, too."

"Well? Go on!"

I licked my lips and glanced around. We were alone in the library. Carefully I shut the door, then drew up a chair and sat facing my father.

"I had a dream," I said. "I need to know what it means."

"Tell me," he said. "Perhaps I can interpret it a little. Though Freda is the one you should ask . . ."

"No. There was a woman —"

"A-ha!" He chuckled. "One of *those* dreams!"

"Shut up and let me finish. Her name was Queen Moins. Have you never heard of her?"

"Moins?" He shook his head slowly, eyes distant. "No. I do not believe so. Who is she?"

"She was the one I saw about last night." Quickly, I told him about my dream, her instructions to remove the Pattern . . . and how real it had all seemed. The fact that I had awakened soaked with sea-water still disturbed me.

"Odd," he murmured. "So real . . . and yet a dream. I would say, my boy, that you fell victim to a spell. Queen Moins must be a real person, though whether she lives here or in another Shadow — or even in Chaos — I cannot say. Beware of her, and of her powers. That is my best advice right now."

"What about the Pattern? She said it had appeared there, and she wanted me to remove it."

"It could mean anything. It might even be a trick to lure you from the safety of Amber."

I nodded slowly. That made sense.

"Then what do you suggest?" I said. "How can I stop her from entering my dreams?"

"Do not go to sleep."

I laughed. "Easier said than done."

"I *do* have an elixir you might try . . ."

"Absolutely not!" I had seen enough of his inventions to think better of trying one out on myself. "Any other ideas?"

"Let me think on it. Meanwhile . . . wear your sword to bed, just in case you wind up in the water again."

Trumpets began to sound outside, a fanfare this time. I glanced toward the door. This had to be the official welcome for Lord Dire.

"He's here," I said. Might as well get it over with. Perhaps Lord Dire would be as useful as Freda seemed to think. The gods knew we needed more allies . . .

Dad rose, too. "We must not keep your guests waiting," he said with a half smile. "It has been a long time since I have seen my old friend . . ."

NINE

By the time we reached the courtyard, Lord Dire's entourage had reached the castle. The soldiers had dropped back, allowing the procession of fancy carriages drawn by large, scaly creatures that somehow reminded me of cats to enter before them. From the foremost carriages emerged a small army of servants dressed in a sickly-colored green-and-yellow livery. They scurried about, some talking with our servants, others unrolling a long, pea-green carpet in front of the final and most ornate carriage.

Hardly an invading force, indeed. Lord Dire's men-at-arms even had the good sense to wait outside the castle. If Dire proved harmless, then I might invite them in.

Dad and I joined Conner and Freda. They had both retreated to the top step of the main audience hall. Freda watched Dire's bustling servants with a definite air of satisfaction.

"You're enjoying this far too much," I said.

"Of course. Lord Dire is a stickler for protocol. Everything must be *just right* for him to make his entrance."

"I'm already bored," Conner said, pretending to yawn.

"Be quiet," Freda told him. Then she turned to me and said, "Stand up straight. Look regal. Protocol is important in Chaos. Lord and Lady Dire must see you looking both strong and healthy."

I raised my eyebrows. Strong and healthy? A curious turn of phrase, and I didn't like it. Conner had been right — she *was* up to something.

"What, exactly, did you mean by that?" I asked.

"I meant what I said. Lord Dire must see you. Nothing more at this time. I will broker our negotiations."

Broker? Negotiations? I glanced at Conner, who looked as perplexed as I felt.

"I want the truth," I said uneasily. "What have you done . . . or agreed to?"

"Their family, like ours, is out of favor in the Courts right now. We need allies, Oberon, and Lord Dire is powerful. With this union, both of our houses will become stronger."

"Union?" Slowly it came to me what she had done. "You mean . . . a marriage?"

Conner gasped. Our father laughed and slapped me on the shoulder.

Freda patted my cheek gently. "It was a pleasant bit of matchmaking, if I do say so myself. Lord Dire's third daughter, Della, has come of age. She seeks a suitable mate. Why not the most eligible man in our family?"

"Not me!" I protested

"Of *course* you, Oberon." She smiled sweetly. "The time has come for you to take a bride and stop dallying with barmaids."

I raised my eyebrows. How did she know about the barmaids? Lena and Merri had both sworn their discretion. Perhaps Freda had seen them in her Trumps; my sister often claimed she could read the future as well as the present in her cards.

"I don't need a matchmaker," I said. Let her find a husband for herself if she wanted a marriage in the family. "When the time is right, I will find my own wife."

Her face grew stern. "No king should ever choose his own bride, including you. After all, what do you know of marriage or matchmaking? Nothing!"

"I know what I want in a wife better than you do!"

"Besides," she continued, ignoring me, "there are ancient traditions to uphold. This is how the kings of Chaos find suitable queens."

"I am no king of Chaos," I snapped. Turning, I stalked inside. "Send the Dires back home with your regrets. You have wasted their time. I will *not* marry some six-legged, half-octopus daughter of theirs!"

"Della is nothing like that!" Freda protested, pursuing me inside. I turned into a corridor, stomping toward my rooms. Servants bowed low as we passed. "In the Courts of Chaos, she is considered a rare beauty!"

"She's beautiful?" Pausing, I thought back to the weeks I'd spent in the Courts. I had seen hundreds of women there, but "beautiful" was not a word that came to mind to describe any of them. Frightening, yes. Strange, undoubtedly. Insane, quite often. But beautiful?

"You must meet her," Freda said in reassuring tones. She took my arm and gently tugged me back toward the courtyard. "The Dires have made a long, hard journey through countless Shadows to see you. It would be rude to disappoint them. And you are not a rude host, I know."

"You should have warned me," I grumbled.

"How? You have been gone for three months! And last night, you never returned to the library."

"Yes, but . . ." I frowned. Perhaps she had a point — not that I would concede it. I shrugged helplessly. "Even so. I do not like surprises."

She folded her arms stubbornly. "Oberon, you are a king now. You must marry and produce heirs as soon as possible. You cannot remain without issue. Think to the future of Amber. Who can you trust but those of your own blood . . . those who also hold the Pattern within them?"

I snorted. "Considering our family and its history, any children of mine are more likely to kill me than all the armies of Chaos put together!"

"That is not fair. Father never had a more loyal right-hand man than Locke." He had been my oldest brother . . . killed by Swayvil's army of hell-creatures years ago, defending our family's keep in a Shadow called Juniper. "Or you," she added.

"Don't forget Aber."

"Aber was a fool. And Father never trusted him."

"Born half of Amber and half of Chaos," I murmured mostly to myself. "What sort of bastard offspring will such a union produce? Will they be monsters or men?"

Freda smiled. "You too are born of Chaos, dear boy. Never forget your birthright. You may have been raised alone and in a distant Shadow, but the fire and steel of true Chaos still lies within your heart. You *will* meet Lord Dire, and you *will* marry Della Dire. It is necessary.

We both know it."

I hesitated. She did have a point. No king should be without heirs. What would happen to Amber and the Pattern if I died? Who would succeed me? No one else would have been able to use the Pattern against the Feynim's creature the way I had. . . .

Slowly I asked, "Are you sure she's beautiful. . . ?"

"Yes." Freda smiled, knowing she had won. I knew it, too, much to my regret. "Dozen of Lords of Chaos have tried for her hand, only to be rejected as unsuitable by Lord Dire. Her beauty and grace are remarkable to behold. Truly, Della Dire is worthy of a king . . . of *you*."

"You didn't answer my question!"

"She has the most beautiful dimensions I have ever seen. Now come."

"*Dimensions?*" I asked. What did she mean by *that*? "Freda —"

Before I could question her more, though, she swept back into the hall. I had to jog to catch up.

"Freda — answer me! What's this about her figure?"

"Later, Oberon!" she called over her shoulder. "There is no time for that now!"

We rejoined Conner and Dad just as Lord Dire's servants formed an orderly line off to one side. One elderly steward remained, standing beside the Dires' coach. He placed a small step by the door, then glanced at Freda, who nodded once.

"Wait here," Freda said to me. "You must not speak to Lord or Lady Dire until my negotiations are complete. Yet both must be able to see you."

"Am I some slab of meat on display in a butcher-shop?" I complained.

"Yes. Now be still. I have work to do."

"When do I see Della Dire?"

"Not today. These things take time."

"As long as I *do* get a good look at her," I said. "And she better be beautiful!"

"Trust me!"

Every time someone said 'trust me,' I always had cause to regret it. My sense of foreboding returned. What had I gotten myself into?

Freda walked forward slowly and regally. As the steward opened the carriage door, the breath caught in my throat. I leaned forward, eager to glimpse Lord and Lady Dire. Perhaps Della would take after her mother —

Then I pulled myself back. Better to be cautious and reserved than over-eager, after all. It might hurt Freda's negotiating position.

The first person to descend from the carriage was a man, and not a very remarkable one by the standards of Chaos: short, stout, with a pushed-in face and steel-gray hair. He dressed all in green, from his dark hose to his lighter-shaded tunic to his gloves to the jaunty little cap on his head.

An intricately jeweled sword hung at his left side from a black belt. A jolt of recognition ran through me. This was the sword from my vision.

It was a beautiful weapon by any standard, though it looked far too heavy for anything other than ceremonial use. Still, like me, all the Lords of Chaos I had thus far encountered had proved far stronger than they looked. If Dire had enough muscle to wield it properly, the weight might not be a problem. Lord Dire comported himself with a quiet dignity, and yet he still radiated a sense of real authority and power. He seemed nice enough. And certainly not the hideous creature I had half expected. If his daughter took after him, she might not be so bad.

And, if the sword was meant to be mine, maybe I had to marry his daughter . . .

My gaze kept returning to his sword at his hip. What must it feel like? I wanted very badly to hold it.

Barely glancing in my direction — just enough that I knew he had taken me in and sized me up — Dire turned to the carriage and extended his arm. A finely-boned hand appeared, pale as new milk. It had to belong to Lady Dire. The breath caught in my throat. She gripped her husband's fingers with delicate grace and eased long, slender legs out. She wore deep green slippers covered with emeralds and green stockings that extended past her knees, quite elegant, quite appealing.

I licked my lips. If Della took after her mother, I might have nothing to worry about. She might even be beautiful, as Freda claimed —

One foot touched the top step with rare grace, then the other. Her tight, calf-length dress, the same green as Lord Dire's shirt, accentuated her curved hips, slender waist, and small, high breasts. Hundreds of emeralds sewn into the fabric winked and sparkled in the sunlight. She was remarkable by anyone's standards.

Swallowing hard at an unexpected lump in my throat, I smoothed back my hair and straightened my crown and clothes. Freda should have given me more warning. With time to prepare myself, I could have taken a sweet-scented bath and gotten a shave and haircut from the castle barber. And I could have ordered richer, more kingly robes from the tailor. It wasn't every day I met my future parents-in-law!

Carefully, regally, her head turned away from me, Lady Dire descended to the flagstones. She moved with an almost sinuous ease.

Slowly she raised her head, murmuring what must have been words of thanks to her husband. That slender, milk-pale neck tilted as she studied the high towers of Castle Amber, still swarming with workers repairing the wind-damage, and for the first time I glimpsed the ivory perfection of her profile. Delicate lips, high aristocratic cheekbones, a slightly upturned nose — she may have been the most attractive woman I had ever seen. If only Della took after her, I would be a very happy man indeed!

Then she turned to look at me. And I could only gape in sudden horror.

Each side of her head had a different face, and they overlapped in the middle. Three eyes, two brown and one gray, blinked lazily at different speeds. Her delicate upturned nose proved to be as broad as my hand was long. And her long, toothy mouth, which extended too far in both directions, gaped into a hideously toothy smile. When a forked, snakelike tongue darted out, I felt the blood drain from my body. I gave an involuntary shudder.

A beauty? A nightmare, rather! How could Freda have done this to me? My heart tightened and my legs turned weak.

"Steady there, boy," said my father in a low tone. He clamped down on my shoulder with an iron grip. "Quite a woman, isn't she?"

"Dad!" I whispered. I wanted to turn my head and look away, but I couldn't rip my gaze from that awful face. "She . . . she's . . ." I could only stare hopelessly.

"Incredible?" My father chuckled, and I couldn't tell if he was mocking me. "She *is* a gem, Oberon. She broke many hearts when she married Lord Dire. I courted her myself, you know, but her father had bigger plans for her."

"Are you *blind*?" I demanded, turning to face him. I couldn't believe he found that awful creature appealing.

He tilted his head as though puzzled. "What do you mean?"

"She's hideous!" I cried.

"Curb your tongue!" he said sharply. "The Dires may be out of favor in Chaos right now, but their family *is* quite powerful. I see why Freda has arranged this match, and she is right. The Dires have many connections we can use. We *need* them — as much as they need us. The fact that all the women in their family are so beautiful is a happy stroke of luck for you."

Beautiful? I just stared at him, bewildered.

Then he slapped my back and leered a little. "Were I a little younger, I might pursue Della Dire for myself! Hopefully she takes after her mother!"

"I wish I were in your boots," Conner breathed softly.

"You're both welcome to her." I set my jaw stubbornly. "I'm not marrying anyone — a 'rare beauty' or otherwise!"

"You will do as you are told," Freda said. "Now be quiet and wait here until I return. I must welcome them properly and officially to

Amber."

She walked out toward the Dires at a casual, unhurried pace. She was enjoying every minute of it.

"I'm *not* marrying Della Dire," I growled at her back.

"Listen to your sister," Dad said. "She knows what is best for you and for Amber."

I looked at him — this gray-haired, wizened little dwarf of a man — then gave a sharp bark of laughter. Who was he to give *me* orders? He might have drawn the original Pattern, but *I* bore its design upon my soul. In the greater scheme of things, his task was done while mine had only just begun.

"You forget yourself," I told him. I deliberately did not call him Dad. "*I* am king here, and I will follow *my own* counsel, not yours — and not Freda's — whenever it suits me."

He seemed to wither beneath my angry stare. All his threats and arguments died away. He must have seen they would prove useless. My heart and my mind were already made up.

In a strained voice, he said, "As you wish, my boy. As you say, you are the king."

"Good." I gave a satisfied nod. It was high time they realized who ran things here.

And I refused to feel guilty about putting him in his place. My father had lied to me for years about my heritage, after all. He had manipulated me like a pawn in some great game. *No more*, I had sworn, and *never again*!

And the same went for Freda. She could be just as bad.

My sister reached the Dires. She hugged Lord Dire warmly,

kissing his cheek, then embraced Lady Dire; clearly they all knew each another, and quite well from the look of things. Which made what I had to do all the more difficult. I liked my sister a lot, and I hated to disappoint her.

Linking arms with my hideous mother-in-law-to-be, Freda escorted her to the right, toward the west tower. Servants began unloading trunks, boxes, and all manner of other possessions. From the sheer quantity of baggage, it looked to me as though the Dires planned on a very long stay.

"I am not unreasonable," I told Dad in a calmer voice. Now that I had made up my mind, I could be perfectly rational about it. "I won't make Freda send the Dires away outright. But you must tell her the answer is no — I will not marry Della Dire. Of course, they are welcome to enjoy the hospitality of Castle Amber as long as they wish. But I have no intention of marrying their daughter."

"You have not even seen her!" Conner protested.

"Don't you start, too!" I said. "I don't have to see her. I've seen her mother. That's enough."

"Your loss," Conner muttered.

"So be it," Dad said, "though your decision may doom us all."

I had to laugh. "Not another doom, Dad!" I had heard that hoary old warning far too many times over the last few years. It seemed that every crisis would lead to our family's ultimate downfall. "Isn't that four dooms this week alone?"

"Do not mock me, boy," Dad said darkly. "Swayvil fears Amber and the Pattern more than you realize. Every day he studies new ways to destroy you and the Pattern. Eventually he will come up with a plan and act upon it. A blood tie to Lord Dire's family might well keep us alive, if it comes down to war again."

"So you say." I shrugged. "Don't forget, though, that we won the last battle against Chaos. We aren't doing so badly on our own."

"True . . . for now." He met my gaze, and his eyes reflected a real concern. "Here is something else to think on. While you were gone, in just those three months, we found and executed four spies from Chaos. We haven't been able to find out how they are getting inside the castle. It shows how concerned the King of Chaos is about you. He still tracks our every movement."

"And what better way to spy on us than through a new wife? Della would have access to all of us and all of our plans."

"What better way to insure our survival?" Dad leaned close. "If I know her father, Della Dire has been raised in the strictest traditions of our people. She will honor her new husband. It is our way."

"I still do not see how this marriage benefits me."

"Swayvil may not like Lord Dire, but he recognizes the Dire family's power and influence. Your death at Swayvil's hands would be a grievous insult, and Lord Dire would be honor-bound to avenge you. He is one of the few men in the Courts whose influence might topple Swayvil from the throne. Swayvil will not risk offending him."

I sighed unhappily. "So marrying Della would keep us safe . . . or safer."

"A thousand times, yes!"

I swallowed. Perhaps, for the good of Amber . . .

Conner said, "At least wait until you've seen her before deciding."

"Very well," I said. He had a point; Della might take after her father. "I'll wait."

Dad smiled, and I knew he thought Freda had won. And perhaps she had.

For the good of Amber . . .

TEN

Dinner that night was a formal affair, held with all the ceremony of a state dinner. We feasted in the grand banquet hall, more than one hundred of us, all seated at a long, broad table that stretched nearly the length of the room. I sat at its head, with Dad at my left and Lord Dire at my right. Freda sat next to Dad, and Lady Dire sat next to her husband. Conner sat next to Freda, then various minor nobles from the surrounding lands. Most had been third of fourth sons of dukes, barons, and counts in nearby Shadows — of noble blood, but unlikely to inherit much at home. Conner and I had lured them here with promises of new titles and land-holdings in exchange for their help in settling this new world.

Lord Dire still wore the sword from the morning, and it took all my effort not to stare at it. I longed to see it more closely. I longed to hold it. *How?*

As we feasted on suckling pigs, braised fowl, and roast venison, I forced myself to chat amiably with Lord Dire. His questions seemed on the surface harmless, but carried hidden depth.

"How many people are under your banner?" he asked casually at one point, gesturing to take in the whole of Amber.

"Oh . . . more than I can count." I chuckled. I too could play this game. "At our last battle, we fielded more than a million fighters. Amber is still growing quickly. If we ever have another such battle, I expect to field at least twice as many."

That was quite an exaggeration . . . but given enough time and recruitment in Shadows, we could have raised ten million men. It was the logistics of feeding, equipping, and housing such an army that made it impractical, if not impossible.

Lady Dire hissed suddenly at me. I almost dropped my knife.

"Uh . . . yes, Lady?" I gulped at the bile rising in my throat.

She asked: "Would that be your battle against King Swayvil, Lord Oberon?"

"Yes, Lady." I could think of nothing more to say, so I returned my attention to my plate. Hopefully it made me look hungry rather than nauseated by my future mother-in-law.

Lord Dire, clearly impressed by the numbers I had fielded, had been nodding slowly. Then his eyes grew distant, as if some plan had begun to form in the back of his head.

"My father mentioned something of your own military accomplishments, Lord Dire," I said. Dad *had* said he might be able to topple Swayvil, if the right situation arose. Perhaps I could put that thought into his head . . . if it hadn't already occurred to him.

"Oh?" He preened a bit. "I have done my duty, of course."

Finally I couldn't contain myself any more.

"And I could not help but notice the sword you wore this morning. I hope you will let me examine it more closely. A beautiful weapon, indeed."

He smiled, nodding. "Yes. Quite beautiful. Its name is *Baryn-*

killer. It was forged by Iccarion himself, for the battle against Baryn Boalar during the Ice Rebellion."

My father gasped in surprise, and I glanced at him in amazement. I had only seen him caught so off-guard a couple of times in my entire life.

"Are you sure it is Iccarion's work?" Dad asked, a note of wonder creeping into his voice.

Freda looked from one to the other of them.

"I thought Iccarion's swords were all destroyed in the war with the Feynim," she said. And that too made my ears prick up.

"Not all," Lord Dire said smugly. "This one escaped. I seldom wear it, however. Too many would try to take it by theft or treachery, so I keep it locked away . . . except on very special, very private occasions, such as this one."

"It looks too heavy for any practical use," I said.

Dire chuckled. "It is as light as a feather. I might have wielded it in battle in my youth, had I possessed it then, but old age has taken its toll. Fighting is for the young, I fear, and politics for the old."

"Who is this Iccarion?" I asked. "Why are his swords important?"

Lord Dire turned a puzzled look upon me. "You have neglected your history lessons, it seems, King Oberon."

"Apparently," I said. Iccarion? Baryn Boalar? The Ice rebellion? I had never heard of any of them. "What have I missed?"

My father said, "Iccarion was the greatest weapons-maker ever to practice in the Courts of Chaos, though he only lived to the age of twenty-six. He crafted ten swords in his lifetime, each a masterwork of beauty and design. Iccarion's blades are said to be unbreakable . . . Apparently he worked primal forces of Chaos into them, using a secret technique which no one has been able to duplicate since that time."

"What happened to him?" I asked. "Was he murdered?"

"No." Dire shook his head. "The magics Iccarion used destroyed him. Very little of his body was recovered. What they found . . . well, it was enough to determine that he had died, and quite horribly."

Freda added, "Horrible by Chaos standards is not a pretty thing, Oberon."

"What about these swords?" I asked. Unbreakable, light-as-a-feather swords interested me more than a little. And they had been brought into battle against the Feynim? "What became of them?"

"Most were lost in the war," Dire said. "I know of only two still in existence. One is mine. The other . . ."

"Let me guess," I said with a short bark of a laugh. "Swayvil has it."

He nodded gravely. "It belonged to King Uthor, though he never carried it. Swayvil took it when he seized the throne. He has been seen wearing it in public several times; apparently he views it as a sign of his power. His sword is called, appropriately enough, *King-maker*."

Somehow, that figured. Could *King-maker* be the sword from my vision instead of Dire's *Baryn-killer*?

"To the victor . . ." I said, musing on the possibilities.

"Speaking of victory," Dire said, leaning back in his chair and smiling, "Swayvil was quite annoyed over his army's defeat. Four generals were executed because of it."

"Perhaps he will think twice before attacking Amber again," I said a trifle smugly. "His defeat was, ah, *complete*."

"Brilliantly so." Dire nodded in honest appreciation, and I found myself really liking him. This was a man who understood the beauty of a well executed battle plan.

"Thank you," I said.

Lady Dire hissed, "I heard you fought like a demon, King Oberon. Rivers of blood must have flowed. Magnificent!"

I forced a smile in her direction. "Thank you. Yes, there was . . . ah . . . quite a lot of blood, Lady Dire."

Her sibilant laugh sent chills through me.

Lord Dire said, "That particular loss weakened Swayvil more than he will admit. It will take years for him to rebuild his armies. And decades to win back the support of the rest of the Lords of Chaos."

"He can only blame himself," I said with a modest shrug. "We *will* defend ourselves."

"Oh . . . no one blames *you*, King Oberon. Poor judgment, bad planning, worse execution . . . The fault lies, as King Swayvil has said many times, entirely with his generals."

"Oh?" I raised my eyebrows. "Why not with the king himself?"

"Fault never lies with a king, Oberon! Surely you must know that rule!"

Laughing, I thought back to Joslon. It applied to him as well as his son. It seemed the rule applied to heirs-apparent, too.

I went on, "Swayvil's loss sounds a bit like a repeat of the war against the Feynim."

He inclined his head slightly. "Kings of Chaos often repeat the mistakes of their predecessors." I heard the unspoken, *But I would not.*

"And if you were king?" I prompted.

"I am not king."

This time there was unspoken *yet* at the end of his sentence. Good; clearly he had big plans for the future. I would have to encourage them. A friend of our family ruling the Courts of Chaos . . . that would open up many possibilities. I could see now why Freda thought a marriage to Lord Dire's daughter made sense.

I said, "There is a saying in the Shadow where I grew up: 'Let sleeping giants lie.' Swayvil would do well to remember that . . . as would *any* King of Chaos. Amber makes a far better friend than enemy."

"King Swayvil won't remember, but I certainly will!" Dire chuckled low in his throat. "And what better way to guarantee peace and friendship than through the marriage bed?"

His wife made another soft hissing sound that might have been more laughter. It made my skin crawl. As I looked her way, another shiver went through me. All this talk of magical swords had made me forget my impending doom for the moment. Now all my dread flooded back. What must their daughter be like?

"Indeed," I said. "I . . . look forward to the union of our houses."

"As do we all."

"I truly would like to see your sword, Lord Dire," I said again, my hint perhaps too obvious . . . not that I cared at this point. "Its history fascinates me. Are you sure it weighs so little?"

He hesitated but a moment. Then, slowly and rather reluctantly it seemed to me, he pushed back his chair and stood. Smoothly he drew *Baryn-killer* and offered it hilt-first.

I rose and accepted it. As he said, it felt light . . . unnaturally light, as if it weighed almost nothing. When I raised it over my head, turning the blade so it gleamed, an almost unbearable joy swept through me. *This* was a blade made for fighting. If I carried such a weapon into battle, I *knew* I would be unstoppable. Let King Swayvil and all the legions of Chaos stand against me. I would slaughter them all!

And yet . . . now that I held it, I realized this one *wasn't* the sword from my vision. Very close . . . but not quite right.

And that meant I was destined to have Swayvil's *King-maker*. I swallowed hard. *How?*

Suddenly I realized everyone had stopped talking and turned to stare. Blushing, I lowered the sword. Returning it to Lord Dire was one of the hardest things I had ever done in my life. I *wanted* that sword . . . craved it like nothing else before in my life. But I knew it was not meant to be.

Still standing, Lord Dire sheathed *Baryn-killer*. Then he picked up his goblet, raised it high, and called loudly: "To King Oberon and Amber!"

Everyone dutifully rose, raised their goblets, and repeated, "To King Oberon and Amber!"

I smiled down the length of the table. Time to score my own points with the Dires.

Raising my goblet, I added, "And to the mother of Amber's first queen . . ." The words caught in my throat, but I managed to squeeze them out. "To the . . . *beautiful* . . . Lady Dire!"

Once again Lady Dire turned her horrible gaze upon me, thin forked tongue flickering across her pale lips. All three eyes blinked and fluttered almost coyly. Was she . . . flirting with me? In front of her husband?

I hid my distaste by closing my eyes and taking a long swallow of wine. Hopefully Della Dire didn't take after her mother's side of the family. And, even if she did, I could probably drink enough to make her passable. At least in the dark, on a moonless night, with the curtains drawn and the lights snuffed out. I hoped.

Just then, as if on cue, rescue arrived. A page in red livery appeared at the doorway — Jobe. Had two hours passed already? I had been using Jobe to arrange trysts with barmaids from the town next to Castle Amber for the last year or so . . . and tonight he would provide an excuse for my escape.

I gave a subtle nod, and he hurried over. He cupped one hand to his mouth and whispered in my ear.

"I am here as instructed, Sire." He spoke so softly, no one else heard.

"Yes." I frowned as if some important state secret were being imparted. "Go on."

The page continued: "Do you want me to do anything else now, Sire?"

"That will be all, Jobe." I waved him away. Without a backward glance, he scooted from the hall.

Forcing a heavy sigh, I rose.

"Is something wrong?" Lord Dire asked, studying me carefully.

I spread my hands, a gesture of helpless apology. Though I had been enjoying Lord Dire's company, I wanted the banquet over. Bad enough to even consider marrying Della Dire; I could not stand to see Lady Dire's face or hear her awful hissing laugh another minute.

"I'm afraid a problem has come up," I said, "and it requires my immediate attention. I will leave you in my father's capable hands for the rest of the meal. I trust you won't mind, Dad?"

"Put it off," my father said. His icy tone told me he had seen through my little ruse. Well, let it annoy him — he could play host just as well as I could, and probably better. After all, as a Lord of Chaos, he had far more in common with Lord Dire than I did.

"I wish I could," I said, smiling through my teeth. "Unfortunately, I cannot let important matters of state go unattended, Dad. You know that." I turned gave a short bow to the Dires. "It has been a memorable and thoroughly enjoyable evening, Lord and Lady Dire. Please, continue your meal. Our cook's deserts are always worth the wait. And there are a few entertainments coming up . . . jugglers, acrobats, and even a visiting poet from Kyar. And perhaps you will have drinks afterward in the library?"

Lord Dire nodded. "With pleasure, King Oberon. I hope you will be able to rejoin us."

"I will try."

Turning, I walked slowly and calmly to the door and into the hall. Once beyond sight of my guests, though, I began to run.

I didn't know where or why . . . but I had to get away. If I heard Lady Dire's hissing laugh one more time, I would have had to kill somebody.

Probably her.

ELEVEN

or the next half hour, while the banquet continued without me, I wandered the castle without aim or purpose, not knowing what to do or where to go. Lady Dire's hideous face kept returning to my mind. What had Lord Dire been thinking when he married her? Blind drunk in a whorehouse, I would not have taken a creature with three eyes into my bed. Even the simplest of soldiers has his limits.

And a king . . .

I wanted more from my bride. I *deserved* more.

Gods, for the old days, when I had been a simple soldier, with simple duties, unaware of my true heritage — unaware of the Pattern! I had been free to live and love, to fight and roam, to truly be myself. Those had been the happiest times of my life.

Then my thoughts returned to Lord Dire's sword. I could see it gleaming in my hand as I raised it to the light. I could feel its uncanny lightness, the sense of sheer *power* it gave me.

More than anything else, *I wanted that sword!*

Perhaps Freda could negotiate it as part of the dowry. Perhaps Lord Dire would make me his heir, in time, and pass it down to me. Perhaps . . .

Slowly, with no real destination in mind, I found myself climbing toward the highest point of the castle, the unroofed south tower that would — if all went as planned — eventually house guest quarters. Repairs were already well underway. Scaffolding covered the roof where tiles had blown off, and more than half of them had already been restored to place.

I climbed out and up. A slight breeze swept in from the north, ripe with the earthy scents of trees and grass and growing things. Our newly-imported farmers would be clearing the forests there soon, readying our first crops . . . planting grapes for the first vineyards . . . fencing off pastures for cattle, goats, and sheep. I hadn't realized exactly how much detail went into building a kingdom when I had decided to settle here and rule. Fortunately, along with the architects and masons we had brought enough bureaucrats to manage the trivial day-to-day affairs without any real input from me.

Sighing, I perched there and gazed out across Castle Amber. Dim lights flickered in hundreds of windows. A haze of smoke rose against the moon and stars from a half-dozen kitchen chimneys. Guards patrolled the battlements, moonlight glimmering softly on their helms and armor. Every now and again they called out the "All's well."

Tonight, everything seemed peaceful and calm. I sighed again. *Trapped.* That's how I felt. Where had the fun of life gone?

I *needed* that sword. . . .

I *needed* adventure. . . .

The wind shifted, and an unexpectedly moist and cool gust from the sea touched my face. Salt and brine . . . a faint fishy smell . . .

For some reason, an image of Della Dire's face as I imagined it might look popped into my head: half octopus, half woman, with three eyes and a snake's tongue . . .

Just what I needed — a reminder of my impending doom. If only I could run away, get back to my old life in Ilerium, be a simple soldier again . . .

I climbed higher, onto the mason's scaffolding, and stood gazing out toward the shoreline. Ships — that's what I needed next. After all, any king worthy of the title had a navy. Could I sail ships here through Shadows? Then, once married, I could be an absentee king for a few years, off scouting new lands and Shadows while Queen Della managed our affairs from Amber. That might be fun!

I knew Conner had already explored the coast for fifty miles in each direction. His scouting party had included a pair of cartographers who had mapped every bay and peninsula. They had found no settlements, no signs of human habitation. But across the water, who could say? It might take decades to map the entire sea. Decades spent away from my hideous squid-bride . . .

I chuckled. Maybe she wouldn't be that bad. After all, my sisters were pretty enough, and they were all women of Chaos. And yet they seemed the exception rather than the rule.

I sighed, shaking my head. As much as I liked to dream, I could never leave this place. Amber was in my blood . . . a part of me, as I was a part of it. You cannot escape your destiny, after all. I would live and love and die here, whatever my secret innermost wishes.

I had just decided to head down to the library for drinks with Lord Dire — perhaps he would let me see his sword again! — when a strange, distant sound reached my ears. The breath caught in my throat. Straining to hear over the faint bustling nighttime noises of the castle, I tilted my head and listened.

It sounded almost like a woman's voice, sweet and low, singing some wordless lullaby. I knew I had heard the melody before . . . so long ago, I could not remember when or where. Had I learned it as a child? Had my adopted mother sung it to me as a baby?

I turned, trying to find the source of the song. Whose voice was that? Where did it come from?

At the edge of the scaffolding, I squinted toward the distant beach. *Out there . . . ?* White sands stretched like a pale, winding ribbon between the dark of the land and the ever-shifting, moon-limned wave crests of the sea. That wonderful voice drifted from somewhere beyond, washing over me like an incoming tide, growing louder and clearer the longer I listened. I could almost make out the words now, and I felt my heart start to race.

Movement in the water caught my eye. Dark, slender figures cut through the waves. Could they be people? Could one of them be singing that strange and beautiful song? I imagined — impossibly, madly! — that I heard laughter as they frolicked in the sea.

That ancient, half-familiar melody continued to stir something within me, something deep and old and powerful. Like a siren's call, it pulled at me. I had to find the singer. I had to go to her.

"Who are you?" I called down, though I knew they could not possibly hear me at such a distance. *"Who are you?"*

Perhaps it was my imagination, but the figures seemed to pause, their dark heads turning slowly in my direction. Then after that moment's pause, their play resumed, and like dolphins they slid through the water once more.

Suddenly unsure, I hesitated. Maybe they *were* animals instead of people. Maybe the moonlight and wine from the banquet were playing tricks on my eyes.

And yet . . . where did that song come from? I still heard it clearly.

Suddenly it didn't matter. That glorious melody rose, loud and strong, and the velvet tones held the cadence of the waves. Light and dark, sound and rhythm, blending and blurring into a wondrous symphony for me and me alone —

"Wait!" I called. I had to see her — the woman singing! I had to find her. I had to have her for my own. "Wait for me!" I shouted. "I'm coming! Wait for me!"

With no thought for my own safety, I raced wildly across the scaffolding even though it rattled and shook beneath my feet. Then I scrambled down the long wooden ladder, through the hole in the roof, and into the tower's storm-ruined upper floor. I burst into a stairwell, pelted down the steps three steps at a time, and raced through long hallways toward the central courtyard.

Sleepy-eyed servants gaped as I passed. Guards leaped to attention and saluted.

I did not care. The only thing that mattered was that song. I had to get to the water as quickly as possible. I had to find that woman!

Into the courtyard, out the side gate, and past the sentries I ran, then onto a rough dirt road that angled toward the sea. The moon provided just enough light for me to navigate around the fallen trees that had not yet been cleared away.

As the ground leveled out, I tucked my head down and let my stride lengthen. I almost flew as I passed a cluster of a hundred or so buildings — mostly houses, a half dozen shops, and two taverns, the beginnings of a town. Lights showed in the windows of Flint's Place and The Skewered Lamb, and both rang with boisterous drinking songs. Off-duty soldiers often found refuge here.

Any other time I might have stopped to join in, but now I barely slowed. Nothing could stop me this night. Nothing could prevent me from finding the woman singing that wonderful old song.

When I reached the beach, that glorious voice rose toward a fevered pitch. My breath came in short gasps and my chest burned. And still I could not stop.

My feet crunched on sand. Across the tideline to the water's edge I raced, and as cold waves broke across my boots I drew up short, staring.

I had not imagined them. The figures in the water were *not* seals. Dozens of men and women played and laughed in the shallows, their glistening, naked bodies like quicksilver in the moonlight. I glimpsed bright flashes of thighs and hips and breasts and faces as they darted this way and that, splashing and frolicking through the waves.

Though I had seen and spoken to almost everyone in the castle and town, I recognized none of these people. *Who are they?* an inner voice asked. *Where did they come from?*

It didn't matter. I found I simply did not care.

Wading out knee-deep, then waist-deep in the water, still I heard that wordless song. Ancient, powerful, it rose and fell across the sea like a living thing, and a terrible longing yawned up inside me. I had to find that singer!

Chest-deep now, I tried to swim and felt myself foundering,

mouth and nose barely clear of the waves. The toes of my boots scraped rocks and sand; my clothes, heavy with saltwater, threatened to drag me under.

Laughing women began calling to me, their sweet voices ringing in my ears like the music of bells: *"Oberon! Come, Oberon! Over here, Oberon!"*

I wanted to be with them. I *had* to be with them.

"Who are you?" I tried to call, but my mouth filled with saltwater. I spat it out, coughing and choking. "Come here! Come to me! I must see you!"

Still the song rose and fell, tugging at my soul. Several of the lithe young women joined me and began pulling off my waterlogged clothing, letting it sink deep into the sea. My boots . . . my knife and sword . . . my belt and pants . . . even my pouch of Trumps disappeared into the depths. Free now, light in the water, I swam towards them. Swiftly they darted away, elusive before my fingers as a morning fog.

Still I called out: "Wait — wait for me!"

I heard more laughter like bells, and suddenly they circled me, joining hands, dancing rings through the waves and water. Still that wonderful, magical melody filled my ears, rising and falling in rhythm with their movement, everything blurring together in a wild and joyous celebration.

"Be free . . . come with us . . . be free . . ."

Finally I understood the words. I began to laugh. Free! Yes, I was free now.

Around me, the water grew warm and buoyant. Soft hands began to touch my arms, my back, my shoulders. Whirling me around like a skiff on a storm-tossed ocean, the women made sport with me, and whenever I reached out to catch hold of one, then another, they darted away like minnows before a net.

Finally, when I grew so tired I could no longer chase them, when I felt my head start to slide beneath the waves, slender fingers entwined my own, drawing me up to the surface again. A beautiful woman's face came close, and once more that wild laughter rang in my ears. As her dark lips came close, brushing mine, a thrilled shudder ran through my body.

I reached for her, and this time she did not draw back, but came willingly into my arms. I kissed her passionately, and once more that electric thrill ran through me. I had never known such an intense feeling before. I never wanted it to end.

As we broke for air at last, I found I could see clearly now. The half moon shone down almost as brightly as the sun. The woman's hair was dark as seaweed, and her skin glistened like fresh silver in the moonlight. She had perfect almond-shaped eyes that glinted like emeralds, high cheekbones, a small upturned nose, and a broad intelligent forehead. When her lips brushed mine a second time, another wild thrill shot through me.

"Who are you?" I gasped out. "Tell me your name!"

Laughing, she darted away. I tried to follow, but more women appeared between us. They took my hands and pulled me farther from the shore. I did not resist much; gazing from one face to another, I found them all equally beautiful, so different from how I imagined my bride-to-be.

Like dolphins we surged across the water, first above then below, that song always in our ears. We held hands and danced. We performed an intricate ballet, while real dolphins and small whales joined us, and the sounds of joyous laughter filled the night.

And still, throughout it all, that wonderful, endless song continued, rising all around us from the sea's floor, binding water and air, flesh and blood. We were one, a joyful union of souls.

The end began with the setting of the moon. The song began to fade. One, then another, then another of the dancers disappeared below the water and did not surface again. Finally only the almond-eyed girl remained. We treaded water slowly, silently, staring at one another. I had never seen anyone more beautiful in my life.

"Who are you?" I asked softly, like a man soothing a spooked mare. She too might vanish if I raised my voice. "What is your name?"

"Braëyis," she said with another laugh. "Catch me, Oberon!"

Suddenly she flipped over and dove deep into the sea, her naked thighs flashing in the pale starlight. Taking a deep breath, I followed . . . down, down, arms reaching toward her elusive silvery form, until my chest burned and my ears ached, and still longer. At last she turned, smiling, and let me grasp her hands in my own. We began to sink toward the bottom of the sea.

At first I struggled toward the surface, but she shook her head. Then her lips were on mine, as hot as my own, and I felt the hard green nipples of her delicate breasts brushing up against the hairs on my chest. We turned slowly in the water, following the currents, drifting ever downward, and I did not mind in the slightest that I would die here.

Her legs wrapped around my waist in a powerful grip. Her fingers tightened in my hair. And still we sank, bodies locked, lips burning together. My lungs began to ache. I broke free from her lips and pointed desperately toward the surface.

"Breathe, Oberon!" she said, and somehow I heard her words clearly. "There is magic in the water. It will taste like sweet air!"

I stopped my struggles and gazed at her delicate face, framed by a billowing cloud of dark hair. She could not possibly lie to me. If she wanted me dead, she and all her friends could have drowned me hours ago.

"Oberon," she said again, hands caressing my chest, "you can breathe. Try it and see. I promise — you will be safe."

Then she took my hands in her own, nibbling my fingers gently. Not only could I understand her under the water, but she seemed to be breathing herself, for her chest rose and fell regularly.

"Trust me," she whispered.

We were a hundred feet down and still sinking. I could never make it to the surface, even if I tried. And yet I could not make myself breathe in the seawater. I looked around desperately.

"Oberon!" she said. "Breathe!"

Trust her.

But how could I possibly breathe underwater?

Suddenly, I didn't have a choice. Opening my mouth, I gasped in what should have been a lungful of cold, murderous saltwater. But I found myself breathing almost normally. My lungs filled with something thicker than air, but . . . it was not like water. And it tasted almost sweet, as she had said.

Magic.

I smiled at her and traced the line of her jaw with one finger, breathing deeply, trying to stop my racing heart.

"Braëyis," I said. "I think I love you."

"Do not tease me."

"You saved my life."

She smiled. "You were never in danger. If Queen Moins wanted you dead, you would already be dead. She has called you here, to her kingdom. She has become interested in you."

"Queen Moins?" I knew that name! I had dreamed of her. "Was she the one whose voice I heard?"

"Yes."

Suddenly I wanted to know a lot more about Moins. She was a real person after all. Did she have a copy of the Pattern, too?

"Tell me about Queen Moins?" I asked. Leaning forward, I kissed Braëyis's neck gently, starting at the curve of her throat and tracing my way to her right earlobe. "Why should she care about *me*?"

"She rules Caer Beatha, the land beneath the waves. You heard her song tonight."

"It was beautiful."

"You will meet her . . . but all in due time. Right now you are *mine*!"

I laughed, pulling away. "Are you sure?"

"Yes!" She drew me close and kissed me again. "Tonight, Oberon, you are *all* mine!"

I smiled but did not reply. Magic or not, with Braëyis in my arms, I had little incentive to return to Amber. Nothing waited for me there but Lord Dire and his hideous wife. And who knew when I might find myself alone with a beautiful woman again?

Grinning, I swept Braëyis close, and our lips and tongues met. Queen Moins' song began again, closer now, thundering through my blood and bones.

Free . . . be free . . . be free . . .

With that strange melody surrounding me, with Braëyis in my arms, I knew such pleasures as few man have ever experiencend.

TWELVE

ime ceased to mean much in the throes of our passion. It must have been hours later that Braëyis finally drew me back to shore and let me go. I stood with her, waist-deep in the water, small waves surging over us, running my hands over her smooth, cool skin.

Finally she drew away, swimming backwards, and she laughed with honest delight when I gave chase. I caught her foot, pulled her back, and once more kissed her cheeks and eyes until she cried out for me to stop.

"I must go now!" she said.

"I must see you again!" I said. "When?"

"Come tonight," she said, touching my chest with her hand. I noticed for the first time that her fingers had a fine webbing between them. No wonder she moved like a fish in the water. "I will wait for you."

"Until the night, then!"

I waved. She swam away, ducking beneath the waves. Her toes broke the surface one last time, then she was gone.

Suddenly exhausted, I turned and waded ashore. Luckily dawn had not yet broken. I'd have enough trouble explaining to Dad and Freda where I'd gone last night after abandoning them at dinner. Half the servants and guards must have watched me run from the castle like a man possessed. If they saw me troop back in naked but for dried sand and salt and seaweed, I knew I'd be the target of jokes for years to come. "The night Mad King Oberon went swimming with the mermaids," they'd call it.

Then I realized I hadn't met Queen Moins. I had allowed myself to become so distracted by Braëyis and the other swimmers that I'd never found the source of that song. Next time, I would have Braëyis take me to Moins first. Then we could satisfy our own lusts later, as time permitted.

I made it to land and threw myself down above the tide-line. My breath came in hard gasps. This had been one of the most exhausting nights of my life, and one of the most intensely pleasurable. Braëyis had been a great lover, as passionate and spirited as any I'd had. My every muscle ached in a good way, as if I'd just had an especially hard workout. If only I could pick a queen like *Braëyis* . . .

The hiss of waves washing onto fine powdered sand filled my ears now, along with the low hum of insects in the grass beyond the dunes. My eyes closed to slits; I clung to memories as a drowning man might cling to a bit of driftwood.

Finally, with a heavy sigh, I picked myself up, dusted the sand off my arms, legs, back, and buttocks as best I could, and headed toward town. My Trumps had disappeared in the water, along with my clothes. The only way back seemed to be on foot.

Maybe I could stop at one of the taverns and "borrow" some poor drunken soldier's uniform first. It would prevent uncomfortable questions and speculations back at the castle if I showed up clothed.

*   *   *

I prowled through all the streets and alleys in town before giving up in disgust. Tonight of all nights I could not find a single drunken soldier to roll for his uniform — my army's discipline seemed, unfortunately for me, quite strong at the moment. Both taverns had already closed, and not a single man lay unconscious on the steps or slumped in a nearby doorway. They just didn't make soldiers like they used to.

Finally, as I circled behind Flint's Place for the third time, I spotted something better than a passed-out soldier: Myrna Flint's laundry. The tavernkeeper's wife had left her wash on the clothesline overnight. I walked along examing dresses, undergarments, kids' clothes . . . and finally shirts and pants belonging to Old Flint himself.

Flint was a big, boisterous man with a booming laugh and a ready flagon of beer. A retired soldier, he stood nearly my own height, though his muscles had long since gone to fat. His clothing would be far too large, of course, but even so, it was better that than nothing.

I slipped one of his shirts over my head. It hung like a tent, the tails hanging down almost to my knees. Then I tried on pants large enough for three of me to stand inside, and those I belted with strips torn from the end of a sheet. I found no shoes or boots, of course, but I could hoof it back in bare feet easily enough.

At last, whistling happily, I started up the road toward the castle again. I was halfway there when I felt a faint sense of contact at the back of my mind. Someone was trying to reach me with a Trump.

I shook my head ruefully. Great timing, as always. Why couldn't they have called me half an hour ago?

I opened myself to the Trump, and suddenly I saw my father in his workshop. His eyes narrowed as he took in my ill-fitting costume.

"I will not ask where you have been or why you are playing dress-up," he said, "but you should know that Della Dire's entourage will arrive this morning. At the very least, you might want to show up for your own betrothal ceremony."

"I'll be there," I said. "Bring me home?"

"Oh, very well!" He reached out, then pulled me through to join him.

"Thanks," I said, looking around.

As always, Dad's workshop was a cluttered, claustrophobic mess; he had wasted no time in reassembling his vast collection of magical objects, scientific curiosities, and odd tinkerer's tools. Mummified cats, the claws of dragons, and other, less readily identifiable objects filled shelves. Bottles labeled everything from "toadstool powder" to "manticore spleen" sat on top. Mostly, though, the room held paper — books, scrolls, and bits of parchment lay scattered on every available surface and piled waist-high in the corner. We might just as easily have been in his rooms in Juniper or our family estates in the Courts of Chaos.

I turned my attention back to my father. He was frowning as he looked me over. Barefoot, encrusted with dried salt and sand, I must have made an especially pathetic sight.

"I have some interesting news," I said, flopping down in the one empty chair. "It seems we're not alone in Amber after all."

"There are other people?" he asked.

"Yes, and they live in the sea. They have webbed hands and can breathe underwater."

He paused. "Are they dangerous?"

"I'm not sure. Their queen, Moins, uses magic. She cast a spell to lure me down to the water. She seems very powerful."

"What did she want with you?"

I frowned. "I'm not sure yet. I'm supposed to return this coming night."

"Freda must hear this." He went to a bell-pull and rang for a servant. A dour-faced teenager I had seen once or twice before appeared from the next room.

"Yes, Master Dworkin?" he asked.

"Tell my daughter Freda to join us," he said. "Something has happened and we need her counsel."

"Yes, Master Dworkin," the boy said, and off he ran.

"I'll be right back," I told Dad, rising and starting for the door. "It will take Freda a few minutes to get here. I'm going to clean up and change my clothes."

"A very welcome idea," he said. "You stink of dead fish!"

By the time I returned to his workshop fifteen minutes later, washed up and wearing a properly fitted shirt and pants again as well as soft shoes, I found Freda waiting with our father. She looked rumpled and out of sorts at having been awakened, but she made no comments or complaints.

Dad's servant had cleared one of the tables, setting out several bottles of wine as well as plates of dried fruits and small cakes from the kitchens. I helped myself. Suddenly faced with food, I found I had a ravenous appetite.

As Freda poured wine for everyone, between bites I launched into my story. It sounded fantastic — even to me! — that a civilization of web-fingered humans could exist beneath the waves, and exist so well hidden that we had not once suspected their existence.

"You said Queen Moins used magic to draw you from the castle," Dad mused. "The song you heard . . . it must have been part of a spell."

That made sense. I nodded slowly. I *had* felt an overwhelming compulsion to find her as soon as I heard it.

"What do you think?" I asked Freda.

"It is . . . interesting." She sipped her wine slowly. "And yet it makes sense. Why else would you leave dinner with the Dires, if not for that spell?"

I shifted uncomfortably. Why indeed. Let her think the spell had done it. She didn't need to know my unreasoning dread of Della Dire.

"You must see this Braëyis again," Dad said slowly, his eyes distant. "And by all means you must speak with Queen Moins. But you must not lose your head over them. Keep telling yourself the song is nothing but a spell. You should be able to overcome it."

"Is that safe?" Freda asked him. "If Oberon cannot control himself around her . . . if he goes willingly into the place of their greatest power . . ."

"I can control myself," I said. "And yes, I *will* go back. I want to see Braëyis again. And I want to meet Queen Moins. She may prove a valuable ally against Chaos, if she's as powerful as I think she is."

Dad nodded. "Do not go alone," he said. "Divide her attention. Divide her power."

"You don't want to come with me, do you?" I couldn't imagine him swimming naked in the sea or frolicking with Braëyis and her friends.

"Certainly not!" he said. "I will be here to rescue you, if you find you need help."

"How about Conner?" Freda said.

I nodded slowly. Yes . . . Conner might enjoy a little seaside romp. It would do us both some good to get away from the castle — and the Dires.

And Braëyis . . . I longed to hold her again. She *was* the most beautiful woman I had slept with in quite some time. I felt my manhood stirring just thinking about her.

"I'll ask Conner tomorrow," I said.

"It *is* tomorrow," Freda said. "The sun is already up."

I glanced at the window. Dad always kept the heavy curtains drawn, but now that Freda mentioned it, I noticed a pale glow spilling around their edges.

"So it is." I turned to our father. "You said Della Dire's coming this morning? Do you know when?"

"Just before noon."

Freda added, "You *will* be here, and you *will* greet her properly."

"Of course!" I grinned. "Would I disappoint my favorite sister?"

"Yes. And frequently!"

THIRTEEN

e retired from Dad's workshop to the dining hall. The cooks had been busy since the early hours of the morning, baking and broiling, roasting and frying, preparing all the day's meals. I found a pleasant selection of pastries, eggs, meats, breads, and fruit already laid out on silver trays. Better yet, Conner had beaten us there and already begun to heap food onto his plate.

"Good morning!" he called.

I replied with a wave.

"You seem unusually cheerful today," I said.

I filled my own plate with eggs, sausage, and some kind of bread pudding, then joined him at the table.

"I don't know . . ." he said, chewing slowly. "Maybe it's just having people from Chaos visiting. I really enjoyed last night. Lord Dire is a great storyteller. You should have joined us in the library. We were there half the night, and I don't know when I've had more fun!"

I nodded, thoughts returning to Lord Dire's sword, *Baryn-killer*. Just thinking about it sent a shiver of anticipation through me. I would have liked to hold it again.

Instead, to change the subject, I told him about Queen Moins and the spell that had brought me down to the sea last night. He frowned.

"I didn't hear anything."

"You were too busy with the Dires. And I don't think she's interested in you; that song was meant for me alone. So — what do you say? Will you join me tonight?"

"Sure. I'd like to meet that new girlfriend of yours. Della Dire is going to get very jealous if you don't learn to leave your sword in its sheath!"

I chuckled. "I'm not married yet. I'm not even formally betrothed!"

"Still . . ." He shrugged.

"Do you know anything about these Chaos-swords?" I asked him. "The ones Iccarion made?"

"Who cares about them? They're ancient history — the stuff of moldering legends. No matter what Lord Dire says, they can't be very good. We lost the war against the Feynim, remember. So much for unbreakable!"

"We don't know if they broke," I said.

"Half the tales about them are probably exaggerations, and the other half lies!"

"If two of the swords made it back to Chaos, do you think there might be more?"

He shrugged. "Maybe. I don't know. Why?"

Licking my lips, glancing to either side to make sure no one could overhear, I lowered my voice conspiratorially.

"I want one."

He grinned. "Lord Dire would have a fit! *Baryn-killer* is his most treasured possession!"

"That's not the one I want."

He stared at me, and I saw realization set in.

"Are you crazy? You want *King Swayvil's* sword?"

"Uh-huh."

"Impossible!"

"Nothing's impossible. Mark my words, one way or another, I'll have his sword!" It was my destiny.

He shook his head. "You're dreaming, Oberon. You have as much chance of that as — as —"

"As founding my own kingdom?"

"Even less!"

I chuckled, but let the subject drop. I could be patient when necessary. Eventually an opportunity would present itself. Whether it be prying *King-maker* from Swayvil's cold, dead hand after a duel, or bribing his valet to swipe it ten years from now, I *would* have that sword. I swore it to myself.

After breakfast, duty called. Accompanied by architects and an entourage of assistants, scribes, servants, and other hangers-on, Conner and I received a tour of the castle. The damage had been fully assessed now, and the news proved better than I had dared to hope.

Fortunately, as already known, most of the fallen débris came from torn-away roofs and roof-tiles; we had gone without significant rain for three months, so the insides of the castle had been spared any water damage. As a result, no floors or interior walls needed to be replaced. In fact, the only real problem was the west tower, which had shifted on its foundations and partly collapsed. It needed to be completely dismantled and rebuilt . . . a task of seven months, no more. The existing stone would be used again, along with the boards and beams.

The castle guard had been helping with the cleanup. The courtyards and balconies now lay completely clear of fallen stones and roof-tiles. Masons and bricklayers already busied themselves patching or replacing everything broken.

Beyond the castle, whole battalions of soldiers had been pressed into service. Mule-teams had begun to clear fallen trees. The logs, once chopped to appropriate sizes and seasoned, would fuel the castle's kitchens for many months to come.

As we left the south tower, trumpets sounded a bright fanfare. Conner and I exchanged a quick glance. Could Della Dire be here already?

Side by side we ran to a balcony overlooking the main courtyard. There, a couple of masons had been replacing broken flagstones. I shooed them out.

Below, a procession of half a dozen carriages drawn by six-legged oxlike beasts pulled slowly through the gates. At the center of the caravan, in an open carriage with gilded posts at each corner, rode a bloated creature with an immense head like a hairy turnip.

Conner and I both sucked in a startled breaths.

That creature (I prayed it wasn't Della Dire!) wore a shimmering white gown that — fortunately — hid most of its body. But from the strange lumpen shapes beneath the material, I could only imagine the worst.

Tentacles.

"Wow," Conner breathed. "She's really grown up!"

The horrible, sick feeling in the pit of my stomach got worse. He recognized her!

Trumpets sounded again. Then a page burst onto the balcony.

"King Oberon!" he gasped. "Lady Freda — says your fiancée — and her entourage — have arrived!"

"Don't tell me it's her!" I gave a curt nod toward the turnip-headed creature, already knowing the answer, already recognizing my doom.

"Yep," Conner said proudly. "That's your bride!"

FOURTEEN

o much for Freda's pronouncements of beauty and grace. And so much for everyone else's tastes in women. Conner was neither mocking me nor making fun of my situation. As far as I could tell, he honestly enjoyed Della Dire's appearance.

"Magnificent!" he kept calling her. "Magnificent!"

I scarcely heard him after the first few seconds. The world narrowed down to just Della and me. It was the sort of moment bards sing about, when lovers' eyes first meet across a crowded room. Just like that, we regarded each across the courtyard, and for that instant time stood still. My breath caught in my throat and my heart jolted heavily in my chest. A shiver passed through me and sweat suddenly covered my body. I felt hot and cold, dizzy and disoriented.

Could this be love?

No! Definitely, positively, emphatically *no*! A thousand times *NO!*

It was *dread*.

The sort of sick, helpless dread a man gets after riding his horse off a cliff, only to plunge screaming for a thousand feet toward certain death on the rocks below.

The sort of dread a man gets when he looks down in the middle of a swordfight to see twelve inches of steel disappearing into his chest.

The sort of dread from which there is no escape. *None.* When all hope is gone and you are looking at a lifetime of exquisite torture from a master of pain — that was the sort of utter *dread* I now felt.

"Magnificent!" Conner breathed.

"Will you *shut up*?" I said, and the moment broke. I could breathe; I could speak again.

"You are one lucky man!"

"I'm not marrying her," I said flatly.

He looked at me, stunned. "What! Are you out of your mind?"

"Look at her!"

"Yes . . . magnificent!"

"Stop saying that! She's the most hideous creature I have ever seen!"

He seemed honestly bewildered. "What!"

"You heard me!"

Freda had appeared in the courtyard. When Della Dire waddled down from her carriage, the two of them embraced. Together, followed by servants and an impossibly large collection of trunks and packages, they entered the castle.

My chest hurt. I wanted to run as far and as fast as possible.

"Now the interesting part begins," Conner said simply.

"Kill me," I said. "Put a sword through my heart!"

"You really don't like her?" he asked. "I know you have a strange sense of humor sometimes, Oberon, but . . ."

Was I the only one who had seen her for what she was? A hideous, lumpy, unwholesome creature?

"No!" I said. "She's hideous!"

He shook his head in disbelief. "Well . . . nothing is settled yet. Freda and Dad will have to work out the dowry and marriage contract. That can sometimes take weeks."

"I get a dowry?" I asked.

"Sure." He shrugged. "Titles, gifts of land and other valuables . . . it all has to be negotiated to the smallest detail."

"Maybe even —" and the word caught in my throat; dared I hope it? — "*Baryn-killer?*"

Conner laughed. "He's not going to give you his sword. Not for marrying his third daughter, anyway."

"Ah."

My lovely turnip-bride disappeared into the castle, trailed by a dozen giggling attendants, each more horrible than the last.

At least Della didn't take after her mother.

Somehow, I didn't find that much consolation.

Negotiations dragged on throughout the morning. I paced the halls like an impatient father awaiting the birth of his first son. Instead of joy, however, I felt a pressing doom. More than anything else, I wanted this marriage called off. But I didn't know how to go about it without offending everyone, from Dad and Freda to Lord and Lady Dire.

Trapped. That's how I felt. Completely and utterly *trapped.*

I retreated to the library, slouched down in an armchair, and proceeded to try to drink my sorrows away. Short of slaughtering everyone in sight, starting with the Dires, many glasses of whiskey seemed the best solution.

At lunchtime, Conner came looking for me. He took one look, then demanded, "What's wrong?"

"Nothing," I said, the words slurring on my suddenly thick tongue. I raised a bottle in salute. "Life is perfect. I'm about to marry a great lumpy turnip of a woman. Long live Della Dire. Hooray."

"Oberon . . ." He gave a heavy sigh.

"I can't stand the sight of her, Conner!"

He blinked. "But — she's stunning!"

"She has a head like a turnip!"

"So?"

"That's not what I want in a wife!"

"What *do* you want, then?" He came and sat beside me. "Her family are all shape-shifters. I'm sure she can find a form more pleasing to your eye, if that's all you want. Have you asked her?"

I shrugged. "It wouldn't be her. I *know* what she looks like now!"

"You're acting crazy. Think of what her family can offer us . . . a stronger position in the Courts. A friendly voice at Swayville's ear when we need it. Perhaps even . . . reconciliation between Amber and Chaos!"

I shook my head. "Forget about Chaos — we can never go back."

"But . . . it's still *home*."

The pain in his voice made my stomach knot up. I knew what he meant. I had felt the same way about Ilerium, where I had spent my childhood what now seemed an eternity ago.

"Chaos can never again be a home for us," I said. "Not after what Swayvil did to our family!"

He shifted uncomfortably. "When you put it that way, Oberon . . ."

"Besides," I said, "we have more pressing problems."

"Like your fiancée?"

I shrugged, then took another long drink.

"Well, what's *wrong* with Della, anyway, other than her appearance being not quite to your liking? She'll make a fine queen. I've always heard great things about her. You don't often get beauty, intelligence, and a sweet disposition. And I bet she's a real tiger in bed!"

I shuddered at the thought. "Somehow, she's just not the queen I envisioned for Amber. I *wanted* . . ."

Then I drew up short. What *did* I want, anyway? I couldn't quite put it into words. But my ideal woman had a thoroughly *human* face, for starters, and she didn't look *anything* like Della Dire.

Braëyis. I wanted someone like her.

"Besides," I said, "We're through with Chaos. What sort of queen would a woman like that make *here*?"

"A useful one," Conner replied without hesitation. "And you know it."

"And what of love?"

"What are you, a poet now?" Conner frowned. "Grow up, Oberon. You're a king. You don't have the luxury of marrying for love or beauty. Della Dire will bear you many fine, strong children . . . many *heirs*."

I shuddered. "Don't even *mention* heirs! The mere thought of bedding her . . ." I rose and began to pace the length of the room. "If you want to know the truth, I can barely stand to look at her! The thought of sharing a bed with that *creature* makes my skin crawl!"

"You need children," he said calmly. "Look how many Dad started with. Now he's down to just us."

"That's not true," I said sharply. "We both know our sister Blaise is out there somewhere." Years ago, she decided she didn't like Amber and ran off to explore other Shadows. "And for all we know, half a dozen others are still alive, too. We haven't seen their bodies. We don't *know* they're dead."

"Maybe," he admitted. "But I think we would have heard something from them if they were still alive. But I'm talking about *you*, Oberon. You're a king now. You need a son . . . there has to be a clear line of succession to the throne. Della Dire will provide that."

"I want something — *someone* — better. Someone I can *love*. By the seven hells, I'd settle for someone I can look at without having to throw up!"

"That's not a king talking."

I strode to the window and spent a long time gazing out at the distant sea. Sun sparkled off the waves. It seemed clean and peaceful out there. That's where I wanted to be right now.

"Maybe I don't deserve to be king," I said slowly. "I miss the old days. I miss the fun. The adventure. And I miss love."

Conner grabbed my arm and pulled me around.

"What's wrong with you?" he demanded. "You're the strongest one in this whole family. You saved us and brought us here. We're depending on *you*, Oberon. We *all* need this marriage. It's for the good of Amber! For the good of *us*!"

"I feel trapped," I said helplessly. "I hate it! I hate everything about it!"

For a moment I thought Conner was going to hit me, but he didn't.

"It's just marriage jitters," he said finally. "You need to get away for a little while . . . have a bit of fun before you settle down. It won't be as bad as you think."

"What do you have in mind?" I asked.

"Negotiations with the Dires will probably last a day or more. Forget about them. We're supposed to go down to meet your mermaid friends tonight, right? Let's do it properly. We'll take a picnic dinner and make a night of it. You'll see, everything will look better in the morning. You just need to get laid."

"That's what *you* think," I growled.

"And," he said, "if you still don't want to marry Della, I'll take care of her for you."

I stared at him, puzzled. "Take care of her? How?"

"Leave the details to me." He grinned wolfishly. "You're not the only one in our family who knows how to get things done, you know."

"Fine," I said. "I'll leave it in your hands. But I warn you . . . if I end up married to that turnip-headed monstrosity, I'm going to hold you responsible!"

"Trust me!" he said. "I have an *exquisitely* cunning plan. . . ."

He had given me enough hope to put aside my bottle and go back to work. Slightly drunk, but not drunk enough to forget Della Dire, I went down to see the architects again and look over plans for the new west tower. They had worked all night drafting them, after all; at least I could get them started on the reconstruction by approving the blueprints.

After an hour of trying to review the paperwork with the architects, I gave up. My head throbbed; my eyes ached. I couldn't focus properly on the work at hand. Here, inside the castle, so close to Della Dire, I couldn't stop brooding over her appearance. Everywhere I turned, I saw that awful face.

Finally I threw all the papers down on the table, rose, and stalked toward the door. "I'll finish tomorrow," I called over my shoulder. "If you can't wait, show them to my father."

"Yes, Sire," they said with just a hint of disappointment in their tones.

I had no clear destination in mind, but I ended up at the stables. My feet had made the decision for me. I might as well take a ride; perhaps I could tire myself out, then take a nap before heading down to the sea with Conner. I still have four or five hours before we were due to leave for our picnic.

"Bring me my horse!" I called to the nearest stableboy, and he dashed off. Two minutes later, he led Apollo out, already saddled and straining at the bit.

Apollo was a seventeen-hands-high warhorse, all black except for one white sock. He was as full of fire and spirit as any horse I'd ever owned.

I swung into his saddle, turned him toward the gates, and gave him his head. He broke for the beach at an all-out, mile-eating gallop.

I still had four or five hours before my picnic with Conner, so I might as well enjoy myself!

We tore down the road, through the town, and over the dunes to the beach. There Apollo slowed to a trot, then a walk. Sweat flecked his hide; he snorted as he spashed through the low waves, kicking up foam and froth. He seemed to be enjoying himself.

We had been riding up the beach for a few minutes when I noticed something white and glimmering in the water ahead. Dismounting, I waded out to see what it was . . . and found myself standing at the top of what appeared to be a long stone stairway extending into the depths.

When I set foot on it, my clothes became dry, as though the water wasn't really water anymore, but that thick undersea air I had breathed last night with Braëyis.

More sure of myself, I descended another three steps. Water surged to my waist now, warm as blood but still dry-feeling. This *had* to be a path to Queen Moins and her kingdom.

Cautiously I eased down a few more steps. The water rose to my chest, then closed over my head. This time I did not hesitate, but breathed — and found my lungs filled with that strangely thick air. When I looked up through the water, the gold of the sun and blue of the sky prismed through the underside of the waves.

Then I looked down to see where the steps led . . . but they stretched farther than I could see, disappearing into a murky green darkness. A line of statues stood to either side, stern-faced men armed with swords and tridents. As I gazed upon them, I had a terrible feeling of having been here before.

Slowly my dream of this place came back. I remembered Queen Moins . . . and her orders to remove the Pattern.

Then I spotted Braëyis climbing slowly towards me and all thought of Queen Moins fled. Braëyis smiled and waved, and I waved back. I leaped down the steps three at a time until I reached her, then pulled her tight and kissed her for a long time.

"Don't forget to let me breathe!" she said, laughing and pulling back. Then she took my hand and led me downward. "Queen Moins is waiting for us."

"Did she make these steps?" I asked.

"They have always been here," she said. "For countless generations, from the dawn of time itself, Caer Beatha has dwelt beneath the waves. There are many paths to it."

"Then why have I never found one before?"

"Because Queen Moins did not wish you to."

More of Moins's magic. I fell silent and let Braëyis lead me down into the green-hued dark.

I felt a small twinge of guilt for coming without Conner . . . but if all went well, the two of us could always return this evening. Perhaps we would have a better time tonight if I met with Queen Moins now.

From the darkness ahead lights glimmered, and a hazy green city came slowly into view . . . Caer Beatha, with its towers and central courtyard so similar to Amber's, and yet *not quite* so. The sprawl of the city around the palace made it hard to see.

Suddenly I realized I was looking at a mirror image of my castle. Everything had been flipped, like a reflection in a looking-glass . . . or in a body of water.

This time, no guards with tridents waited at the gates. Though the streets were deserted, I sensed thousands of eyes peering out at me from cover.

Braëyis escorted me up the central street. Without hesitation she entered the palace, that odd mirror-image of Castle Amber. We entered a long, high-ceilinged room. This would have been the banquet hall at home, but here it had become a throne room. Alcoves holding statues of stern-faced men lined the walls. A chandelier filled with candles burned overhead, though how it stayed lit underwater confused me.

And, at the far end of the room, seated on an intricately-carved ivory throne, sat a handsome older woman. She was tall and long of leg, and she held her pale face high. A sweep of graying hair tinged with green billowed slowly around her head; through it, I glimpsed the gold of her crown. She wore a pale geen gown sewn all over with pearls.

She stared down at me and did not smile. Nevertheless, I gave her my most charming bow. It never hurt to play up to a lady, and if she was anything like the Queen Moins I had dreamed about, I knew flattery would not hurt my position here.

"I am pleased to finally meet you, Queen Moins," I said. I could not help but add, "I have *dreamed* of this day."

At the word "dreamed" her eyes flickered slightly toward Braëyis. Yet she held her tongue.

I continued: "Although I remain puzzled as to why you kept your city and your people hidden for so long, I am pleased to finally meet with you. You will find me a happy guest and — should you return the favor with a visit to Amber — a willing host."

"If you want a reason for your presence," she said, rising slowly and majestically, "consider the ruin you have brought upon my people."

"Ruin?" I said, puzzling on that choice of work. "What am I supposed to have done?"

"You truly do not know?"

I spread my hands. "I have no idea, Queen Moins."

She gestured to Braëyis. "Leave us."

"Yes, Majesty." Braëyis bowed and backed from the room.

To me, Queen Moins said, "Come. You must see what has happened."

Without hesitation, she took my arm and escorted me out through a back door. We passed through several long corridors, descending steadily, until at last we reached a large stone chamber much like the one in Amber that housed the new Pattern. And, as in Amber, here too I found an intricate blue line etched into a plain stone floor . . . only *this* Pattern seemed to be a reversed copy of the true Pattern.

Even backwards, it radiated power. It *worked*, just like the real Pattern. I stared at it, following its unfamiliar sweeps and curves for the longest time.

"It appeared three months ago," Moins said, "just before that dry-world storm. It is my worst nightmare made real, Oberon. Everything has changed in this city because of its presence."

"How so?" I asked.

"My magics are weakened. My power is a shadow of what it used to be. Day by day, hour by hour, I feel control of this world slipping away."

"You still dominate the sea," I said, taking in the whole of Caer Beatha with a sweep of my hand. "Last night, the spell you wove caught me by surprise. It summoned me here. It was the most beautiful sound I had ever heard."

"My powers are strongest by moonlight." She smiled, but sadly and with little humor. "I see the changes all around, Oberon. The old world has ended and a new age has begun. Nothing will ever be the same again. My day has passed."

"Perhaps," I said, touching her arm gently, "the new age will be just as good for you. Perhaps it will be better. For us both."

She looked up into my face, searching my eyes. I smiled and cupped her cheeks in my hands, stroking her skin gently with my thumbs. Then I kissed her, and after a startled pause she responded to my touch.

"You are a very beautiful woman, Moins," I said, drawing back. "My heart — my sword — are yours, freely given. If it lies within my power, I will do whatever you ask. I do not make this offer lightly. You do not need spells to win me over."

"I hoped —" She broke off and looked away.

Softly, I chuckled. I knew what she meant; it had almost been a confession.

"You hoped to win my cooperation through Braëyis," I said. "I know, Moins. I am not a fool. I do like Braëyis, with or without your magics, and I would not trade my night with her for anything. But consider this: what I did, I chose to do. Your spells did not work on me long. I could have broken free anytime, but I chose to stay. I was happier here than in my own home!"

She smiled, and I saw my words had pleased her. We were off to a much better start this time.

"The last time we met, you asked me to remove the Pattern," I began, taking her arm and leading her back toward the throne room.

"Yes. Do you still refuse?"

"If I could get rid of it, I would. I asked my father about it, but he doesn't know how . . . and he *created* the Pattern."

"But why did it appear *here*?" she cried. "And why *now*?"

I shrugged. I would keep my battle with the Feynim's creature to myself for the moment. She didn't need to know how I'd shattered the Pattern defending myself.

"This is an age of great changes," I said. "We have all struck a new balance with the universe. The power of Chaos is waning. Make sure you ally yourself with the right side."

"Your side?" she said.

"Of course." I smiled and winked. "You must already know that the real Pattern has moved inside Castle Amber."

"I neither know nor care. *This* Pattern must be removed. After all, you are its vessel — its stamp is plain upon your soul. You *will* find a way."

"Your faith in me is flattering," I said, "as is my faith in you. I have a proposal."

"Yes?" She looked puzzled.

"Marry me. Unite our lands and people!" *And help me escape Della Dire . . .*

"*Marry* you?" Moins laughed. "Whatever for?"

"I'm serious!" I said. "Why not have the best of all worlds?

Together we would make a formidable team."

Moins clapped her hands twice sharply, and doors to either side of us flew open. From them poured several dozen soldiers, all armed with tridents. Moving fast, they surrounded me. I might have killed a handful, but I wasn't sure I could take so many at once. I glowered at them, though.

"Take him out," Queen Moins said to her men. "Back to the dry world with him!"

So much for my marriage proposal.

Almost before I knew what was happening, I found myself being hustled out the door, back along the city's deserted streets, and up to the white stairway.

"Go on," said the captain of the guard, pointing with his trident. "Stick to the middle of the steps. If you slip or fall, the pressure of the water will kill you."

I did not deign to reply. Swallowing, I began the long climb toward the surface.

I had no idea how long I had been in Caer Beatha, but from the look of the sky above, darkness had already fallen. Conner would be disappointed I hadn't waited for him. But, if it was early enough, we might still make it here from the castle.

Finally I broke through into the air. Night had indeed fallen, though the moon provided plenty of light. I waded up on shore and whistled for Apollo.

As I topped the first dune, my ring pulsed sharply. A warning?

Without hesitation, I whirled and drew my sword in a single swift move. Once more, the spikard had saved me. A dark, silent figure was rushing at me from behind.

"Who are you —" I began

Moonlight caught on steel. A sword whistled straight for my neck.

FIFTEEN

parried, then parried again, our blades ringing like bells off of one another. I gave way steadily before her attack. The thrusts and slashes hammered down on me, and I found myself hard pressed to stop them.

My opponent was a woman. Nearly as tall as me, but willowy, her long pale hair hung loosely around her head, and she wore plate mail on her chest. Her teeth were set in a determined snarl. With the moon to her back, though, I couldn't make out her features.

"Who *are* you?" I demanded, still retreating.

"Murderer!" she growled.

My boots fetched up against something hard; I almost fell on my back. Just barely, I caught myself. But it had thown me hopelessly off-balance. My attacker batted my sword aside, feinted, switched hands, and struck my wrist with the flat of the blade in a move I had never seen before.

The blow stung. Against my will, my fingers spasmed open. I dropped my sword.

Again she pressed her attack. I leaped away, giving up ground fast. How could I protect myself now?

I still had a knife in my belt, so I drew it. The blade barely stretched the length of my right hand, but I felt better holding it. I might be able to turn aside a sword-thrust or two. And maybe, in the dark, I might be able to land a lucky blow of my own . . .

She turned her head fully into the moonlight, and I saw her face clearly for the first time. That thin nose . . . those high cheekbones . . . the sweep of her hair . . .

Her resemblance to me was more than uncanny. She had to be family. *I knew her!*

"Isadora?" I asked my sister.

"Shut up!" she growled.

"Why are you doing this?" I cried.

When she didn't answer, I went down on one knee as if stumbling. Instead of catching myself, though, I grabbed a handful of sand and went into a fast roll. Three sommersaults down the sand dune and I came up on my feet, running hard.

"Apollo!" I yelled. I gave a shrill whistle. But my horse didn't answer, damn him.

Isadora gave chase. Not for the first time I longed for the powers of my brother Aber, who could have pulled a new sword from mid-air using the powers of the Logrus.

I realized I couldn't outrun her. Rather than let her run me through from behind, I turned to face her, my knife out and ready. Then, with a sudden jerk of my left hand, I threw sand into her face.

She hadn't seen it coming. Blinking hard, rubbing at her eyes with her empty hand, she fell back. I closed fast, going for a one-handed stranglehold. This close, her sword would be useless.

Isadora had a few tricks left, though. Even half blinded, she knocked the knife from my hand, kicked the back of my knee, and punched my chest with the force of a battering-ram. I fell flat on my back with a grunt of surprise. Dropping her arm, she stabbed down at me with her sword.

I got my knee up just in time to intercept the blade. Six inches of steel pierced the fleshy part of my calf. Gritting my teeth, I fought back a cry of pain.

Instead, I threw more sand into her face. She pawed at her eyes and spat sand from her mouth. Then I kicked with my one good leg. The heel of my boot caught her stomach, and she doubled over, grunting. I kicked again and knocked the sword from her hand.

I scrambled after it. But she was just as fast. I got there a heartbeat ahead of her. As my fingers closed around the hilt, her hand closed around my wrist. We struggled silently for a second, but I began to pull free.

She must have realized I was stronger. Suddenly she swung around, released my wrist, and kicked me in the chest as hard as she could.

Gasping, the air knocked from my lungs, I sat down hard. I couldn't breathe, could barely think.

She kicked the sword from my hand, then leaped on top of me. From somewhere she had pulled a smaller blade — perhaps four inches long — and tried to drive it into my left eye.

I caught her wrist, took a great shuddering breath, and *pushed*. With a snarl, she pushed back even harder, and the blade slowly descended toward my face.

"Why are you doing this, Isadora?" I demanded.

She did not reply. I tightened my grip on her wrist, fingers digging deep into her rocklike muscles. Bones grated against bones. After a second of this, she gave a mew of pain and dropped the knife.

I let go of her arm and punched her in the face, hard. Then I heaved her off of my body.

Like a tiger, she came up lunging for my throat, fingers outstretched like claws. I batted her hands aside and punched her again, hard enough to hear her nose crunch. *Broken.* Her head snapped back; blood ran freely down her chin.

"You'll pay for that," she snarled.

"Stop attacking me, Isadora!"

"Murderer!"

She seemed to be teetering a bit. But I didn't think I'd hurt her that much — yet.

Then I remembered how nearness to the Pattern first affected my brothers and sisters. It had made them sleepy, as if they had been drugged. The same thing seemed to be happening to her. If I could hold her here while the Pattern affected her —

"Tell me why," I said in a quiet voice. I climbed to my feet, wincing at the burn of pain in my calf, and limped toward her.

She swayed. One hand went to her head.

"What . . . what's happening —"

"Look at me!" I said. *"Isadora!"*

Her eyes opened wider. "Magic —"

She fumbled with a pouch and pulled several things out. A couple of them fell to the ground, but she managed to raise one.

"Light!" she commanded.

A glowing ball appeared between us. I squinted, shielding my eyes.

In the brightness, she looked pale and sick, about to pass out. Her reddish-blond hair fell over her face as she fumbled with a Trump.

"No!" I cried. "Don't!"

She focused on it. I leaped forward — too late.

She disappeared, and the ball of light winked out.

SIXTEEN

sank down on the sand to catch my breath. Spots swam before my eyes. As I blinked hard and waited for them to disappear, I applied a steady pressure to the stab-wound in my left calf. My fingers grew slick with blood.

Where had my horse gone? I whistled for him again, but he didn't appear.

As my eyes grew accustomed to the night again, I noticed the two Trumps she had dropped. Wiping my fingers clean on my shirt, I picked both up. I would check them out when I got home.

I ripped part of my shirt and tightly bandaged the wound. At last the bleeding slowed. Rising slowly and painfully, I picked up a piece of driftwood to use for a cane.

Slowly, I limped toward home. So much for a nighttime frolic with the sea-folk. So much for a pleasant afternoon ride.

By the time I reached Amber, I had lost a lot of blood and felt faint-headed. Even so, I managed to make it to my bedchamber on my own two feet before collapsing.

When at last I awoke, feeling ravenously hungry, day had already broken. Sunlight bathed my bedroom in a warm yellow glow. My leg throbbed. My back and neck ached. I felt battle-worn.

Groaning, I sat up gingerly. New pains blossomed in my left thigh, shoulder, and hip, probably from my tumble down that sand dune.

"How do you feel?" my sister Freda asked. She sat on the foot of the bed, watching my face.

"Alive, at least." I pulled up the sheet and examined my leg. Someone had cleaned and neatly dressed the wound in my calf. I peeled back the bandage. The wound had almost completely healed. But then, I always healed fast.

"Your work, I assume," I said to Freda. "Thanks."

"Who did you fight?"

"Isadora." I detailed our battle on the beach, how tough our sister had been . . . and how she seemed to hate me.

"Odd," Freda commented.

"That's all you have to say?"

"For now, yes."

I snorted. Odd, indeed!

I had only met Isadora once, and then just in passing at a family dinner. I had been so overwhelmed with new names and faces at the time that she had hardly registered. One of my brothers had jokingly called her "the warrior-bitch from hell." The title certainly fit.

Which reminded me . . . Isadora had dropped two Trumps in her haste to escape. What had become of them? Suddenly I wanted to see who or what they showed.

"I had some Trumps —" I said. I glanced around my room, but didn't see them anywere. Someone must have put them away.

"Trumps?" Freda stood, looking around. "I see two on the table by the window."

"Get them for me, please? Isadora dropped them last night. Perhaps they can tell us something."

She crossed to the table and picked both cards up. Rather than giving them to me, though, she raised them to eye level. I saw smudges of dried blood on their backs.

Then Freda paled. Turning, she ran from my room.

"Hey!" I shouted. I had never seen her move that fast before. "Freda! Get back here! *Freda!*"

Throwing off the bedclothes, I climbed unsteadily to my feet. My calf hurt a little, but it supported my weight. I limped as far as the door, then thought better of it. A king shouldn't roam his castle dressed in bandages and undergarments. At the very least, I needed a sword.

Fuming, I bellowed for my valet. He came running.

"Yes, Sire?"

"Clothes, and hurry!"

"Yes, Sire!"

While he retrieved a shirt and pants from the armoire, I sat on the foot of the bed and called for more servants. Two came running from the hallway. I dispatched the first one to locate Freda. The second went to the kitchens; I wanted breakfast ready for me.

Five minutes had passed by the time I was suitably attired in loose blue pants that didn't rub my bandaged calf, a white silk shirt embroidered with baby pearls, and shoes rather than boots. I buckled on my swordbelt.

Then the servant I'd sent to locate Freda returned, panting hard from his run.

"Lady Freda is in the library with Lord Dworkin," he said. "They gave instructions for no one to disturb them!"

Of *course* she went running to our father rather than tell me anything. I should have guessed. They were too much alike, that pair. I needed to work on Freda and get her to confide in me instead.

"Do you have any idea what they are doing?"

"No, Sire." He shrugged helplessly. "They called for tea and cakes, but beyond that . . ."

Tea and cakes? That meant serious plotting.

"Send my breakfast to the library," I growled. "And plenty of wine!"

Fuming to myself, I limped down the hall. By the time I reached the library, I had worked myself into a rage. *I* was in charge here. Freda couldn't abandon me like this. What *had* she learned from those Trumps?

Fortunately, the library door wasn't locked, or I probably would have smashed it from its hinges. I stormed in and found Freda sitting next to our father on the couch, cozy as two little conspirators could be.

"What in the seven hells —" I began.

Isadora's Trumps sat on the tea-table before them. Freda reached out and turned them both face-down.

"About time, my boy," Dad said. "This is important. Get over here!"

Biting back an uncivil reply, I dragged over one of the armchairs and slouched into it, facing them. Just then a servant showed up with a tray of bacon, eggs, biscuits, and honey. Freda smiled; she must have known I would follow her and had taken the liberty of ordering it for me.

I *was* famished. Taking the tray, I growled my thanks. The servant bowed and fled.

"Why are you making such a fuss over those two Trumps?" I demanded, beginning to eat ravenously. "Why did you run off with them?"

"Take a look at this Trump," she said, flipping the first one face-up.

It showed a woman I didn't know — silver-haired but youngish, perhaps in her late twenties or early thirties, with a radiant face. She was dressed all in white and silver, and she held a pair of matched swords crossed in front of her chest. Whoever had painted the card clearly idolized her. And yet her expression had a dangerous edge to it, an almost menacing undertone that made me distinctly uneasy. She was dangerous.

Freda said, "Do you recognize her?"

"No." I felt certain I had never seen her before. Attractive in a way . . . but I had no idea who she might be. "Do you know her?" I asked.

Dad said, "We are not sure. She looks familiar. She may be the daughter of someone Freda and I know. Or perhaps a niece."

"How about the artist?" Freda said. "Do you recognize him from his work?" She leaned forward expectantly.

His work? She must already know who had painted them.

I picked up the Trump and studied it lightly, trying not to make contact with the woman. The card felt cool and hard, almost like ivory, but curiously light . . . lighter than any of the other Trumps I owned. Was it made from something different? I turned it over slowly. Two bloody fingerprints had dried on the back, both mine from the fight on the beach.

"It looks like Aber's style to me," I said, studying the delicate brush strokes. "He must have made it before I killed him."

"We agree," Freda said. "It *is* Aber's work."

"Yes," said Dad. "Aber made it, I have no doubt. And it has been painted within the last month. Maybe within the last week."

"Impossible!" I said. I looked from one to the ot her. "He's dead."

"Are you sure?" Dad asked.

"I cut off his head and buried the body — of course I'm sure!"

"Nevertheless, he painted it, and recently," Freda insisted.

"How can you tell?"

"There are ways. And . . . note that it is an Amber Trump, drawing on the Pattern rather than the Logrus for its power. Someone who has been here and seen the Pattern made it."

"Forget about Aber." I frowned. "Do you think we have another traitor in our midst?"

"Who else could have made it *except* Aber?" Dad asked.

"It wasn't him. It's not possible."

"Give us another explanation, then," said Freda.

I mused through the possibilities. "Someone Aber taught, perhaps? Maybe Blaise?" Our sister was alive, but hiding somewhere in Shadow. "It *could* have been Blaise."

"No," Dad said, "it was not made by Blaise. She has never made a Trump in her life."

He exchanged a look with Freda that I couldn't quite decipher. I examined the Trump again. I might be more closely attuned to the Pattern than anyone else alive, but I still had a lot to learn about its powers.

Ignoring the image, I concentrated on the card itself . . . its substance, the magical forces that bound it together. Slowly I sensed the Pattern contained within the *essence* of the card. It had been made here, all right, using the Pattern.

Unhappily, I set it back down.

"What about the other card?" I nodded at the second Trump on the table.

Without a word, Freda turned it over.

It showed our half-brother Aber . . . but changed. I leaned forward to examine it more closely. His head hung at an odd angle, and the right side of his face now sagged as though he had suffered a stroke. He wore a high-collared shirt with gold braid and buttons, almost military in style. And he had a strange, brooding, intense look to his eyes.

"It can't be him," I said. I tossed the card back onto the table. "It's not possible. This is someone's idea of a joke."

"It *is* him," Freda said. "He *is* alive."

My gaze returned to Aber's Trump. Although changed, the portrait unmistakably showed our brother. I would have recognized him anywhere. And, like Dad said, it looked as though it had been painted just as recently as the first one.

But why would anyone make a Trump of a dead man?

The answer had to be . . . *because he wasn't dead.*

Could I have killed the wrong man three years ago? I frowned. No. I *knew* I'd killed Aber. It had been one of the hardest things I had ever done in my life.

Then another possibility occurred to me.

"Could this be some other sibling no one bothered to tell me about?" I asked. "Maybe Aber's twin brother, out for revenge?"

"No," Freda said. "There are no more of us."

"Aber," Dad continued slowly, "may not be quite as dead as you think."

"What do you mean?" I met his gaze. "I cut off his head. I buried his body! You don't get any more dead than that!"

"Magics may have been worked on the fresh corpse," Freda said softly, touching my hand. "There are some in the Courts of Chaos who follow dark paths. The dead *can* be made to rise, given enough time . . . and enough power. The Logrus can do it."

"What?" The breath caught in my throat.

"Do not blame yourself," she said. "You could not have known about Aber's resurrection. I only know of two others who have been brought back from the dead. Both times, it ended badly for everyone involved."

"Locke . . ." I whispered. The possibilities were staggering. "Davin . . . Titus — the rest of our family! We could bring them all back —"

"No!" Dad said sharply. "Do not even think about it!"

"You must never use this kind of magic," Freda said. "It will consume you if you try."

"But —"

"The results are always tragic!" Dad said. He tapped Aber's Trump with one knuckle, then looked me in the eye. "If Aber *has* been resurrected, he will not be the same man we knew. He will be twisted . . . *evil.*"

I grimaced. "He was already twisted and evil. Maybe death changed him for the better."

"He will be worse," Freda said. "*Far* worse. Whatever morals and loyalties originally steered him will be gone. And his personality will have changed. He will no longer be *our* Aber. He will be some *thing* that looks like him. King Swayvil must have raised him to bedevil you."

Remembering my old king, whose severed head had been left to spy on me when I returned to Ilerium, I swallowed hard. I knew exactly what she meant. Once the hell-creatures finished their work, nothing remained of the kind and fatherly man I had served so willingly. The resurrected king had been an empty shell, a shrill-voiced caricature of his former self.

I looked away. Why did things have to be so complicated?

"Oberon . . ." Freda said.

"What do we do now?" I asked flatly. "Should we try to contact him?"

Freda pushed his card toward me. "You are the king, Oberon. It must be your decision."

"What do *you* think?"

"Contact him," Dad said. He pounded the table with his fist, making my breakfast dishes jump "Track him down. Kill him, whatever it takes!"

"And when next you have his body," Freda said, her face hard, "destroy it — destroy it utterly with fire and steel! That is the only way to stop the abomination he has now become! If you leave his body intact, he may be brought back again . . . and again . . . and again!"

SEVENTEEN

 stared at Aber's card for a long time, then picked it up and turned it face-down. Aber had been my favorite brother until I discovered he had betrayed me . . . betrayed us all. I had known he resented our father; all my siblings lived in a constant state of conflict with *someone* in the family. But I had believed us to be friends. He had been the only one I would have entrusted with any secret . . . with my life itself.

And, in return for my trust, he had betrayed me to King Swayvil.

Of course I had killed him. He hadn't left me any choice. Cutting off his head had been the hardest thing I had ever done in my life. I had wept over his body when the deed was done.

"Well, my boy?" Dad demanded. "What are you waiting for? Get on with it!"

"Not right now," I said. We had other, more urgent business to attend to first. "He can wait. Right now —"

"Your betrothal ceremony," Freda said, nodding. "You are correct, of course. But do not leave Aber too long; he *will* be up to mischief."

"Yes." Mischief . . . hardly the word for it. I had thought my father a master of deceit and obfuscation, but Aber had him beat. I knew I would have to move against my brother, and soon.

But not today. Picking up his card, I stuck it in a pouch at my belt. I would add it to my own deck of Trumps whenever I retrieved them from beneath the sea.

I continued, "Now, about this wedding you've been planning. Send Lord and Lady Dire back to Chaos. I want no part of them or their daughter."

"Consider this match well," said Dad. "Della is from a good family, even though they are out of favor in the Courts at the moment. Lord Dire is ambitious and well connected, and I expect he will soon have Swayvil's ear."

"Then why join his family to ours? We are the enemy of Chaos. Unless . . ." Could Lord Dire be planning to influence me through his daughter? Would that be his path into Swayvil's good graces?

"Look at it from Lord Dire's point of view," said Freda. "You are the one great unknown in King Swayvil's life. Will you attack Chaos? Will you try to seize control of the Logrus as well as the Pattern? You showed your teeth once, when you destroyed his army. He must fear you now."

"And Lord Dire will claim influence over me through his daughter."

"Of course he will." Dad smiled. "Della will offer a voice in Amber sympathetic to Chaos. As your wife, she will have your ear. Swayvil will want to take advantage of that. But it works both ways. Through Lord Dire, you will have Swayvil's ear as well. And Dire will be a voice of moderation."

"I see." I nodded slowly. It did sound as though we would all benefit from this marriage. If only Della Dire wasn't such a horror to look upon!

"At last you understand!" Freda smiled triumphantly. "And Della's dowry will be substantial . . . Lord Dire has already hinted that he will grant you lands and titles in the Courts of Chaos."

"Chaos and Amber do not have to be enemies," Dad said. "Once Swayvil realizes this one great truth, our problems will be solved."

"You forget one thing." Rising, I began to pace. "I don't want her for my bride!"

"Why not?" Freda demanded.

"Her face — her body — she repulses me! I would sooner take a scorpion into my bed. She is a great lumpen turnip of a woman!"

"In Chaos, she is considered a rare beauty," Freda countered.

"Great spirit seldom goes with such magnificent looks!" Dad said. "She *is* a prize worth fighting for."

"Then *you* marry her!" I countered

"If I were only a hundred years younger . . ." Dad murmured with a chuckle.

Unbelieving, I gazed from one to another and back again. Had we looked upon the same woman? Perhaps, because they had been raised in Chaos, they had different standards of beauty than I did. As for me, I could have no part of Della Dire if I could possibly help it.

"You have my decision," I said, rising. "It's final."

"No," Freda said firmly. "It is not."

EIGHTEEN

here was a small garden near the center of the castle where I sometimes went to sit and think. It had white pebble paths that meandered through beds of red, orange, and yellow rosebushes. Other than the gardener — an elderly man who moved from plant to plant with the speed of a snail, constantly snipping, constantly pruning — I was the only one who ever came here.

I sat on a marble bench, stretched out my injured leg, and tried not to brood on my many problems.

A sister who wanted to kill me.

An evil brother raised from the dead.

A queen in an undersea city casting spells on me.

A wedding I couldn't seem to escape, no matter how hard I tried.

The sound of light footsteps on the path brought me back. I glanced up to find the most strikingly beautiful woman I had ever seen walking toward me. Golden hair . . . skin like ivory . . . delicate, almost sculpted features . . . When she smiled, showing perfect white teeth, I felt my heart skip.

I rose, bowing from the waist.

"Good morning," I said.

"Good morning, King Oberon," she said. Her voice, light and

musical, brought a smile to my lips. Here was a woman I could love! Where had she been hiding? Why had I never seen her before?

I gestured toward my bench. "Would you care to join me?"

"Thank you."

She sat, and I joined her.

"You are . . . ?" I prompted.

"Della."

I stared at her. "Della . . . Dire?"

She nodded. I swallowed hard, all my dreams crashing down. Hadn't Conner said she was a shape-shifter? Freda must have put her up to this . . . made her come out to seduce me. It wouldn't work. I knew what she really looked like, beneath this false façade.

"It seems . . . we are to be married." Her voice broke a little.

I couldn't help myself. I reached out and took her hand. Her skin felt as cold as ice, unnaturally cold. This wasn't her real body.

"You don't want to marry me, do you?"

"I am a daughter of Chaos." Her voice had a wistful, distant note. "I know my duty, and I will not disappoint you, King Oberon. If this is how you want me to look, I will keep this form. I know how *hideous* you find my true appearance."

I felt my stomach twist up in knots. The way she said it, the way it sounded coming from those perfect lips, made me deeply ashamed. Perhaps Conner and Freda had been right. Perhaps I had been too hasty in refusing her hand. She truly *was* beautiful now.

For the good of Amber . . .

I swallowed.

I said, "I did not want to marry anyone right now, Della. Freda sprang this on me without warning."

"If you do not want me, send me away." Her dark eyes met mine. And, in them, I saw deep misery. She did not want to marry me any more than I wanted to marry her.

"Is there someone else?" I asked gently. "Someone you love?"

"No," she said, but she could not meet my gaze. "I am thinking only of *your* happiness, King Oberon. I could not live knowing you were displeased with me."

I nodded. "Thank you," I said. She had more depths to her soul than I had guessed. Perhaps she *was* worthy to be my queen . . . and the mother of my children. Could she be a key to my vision of the magnificent future Amber?

Della rose, looking around like a startled deer. "I must go. I should not have come without a chaperone. Good-bye, King Oberon."

Turning, she darted up the path and disappeared around a rose-bush hedge. Distantly, I heard a door bang shut, and she was gone.

Slowly I stretched out my legs. The distant sound of the gardener's shears snipping rosebush leaves reached me.

I had a lot of thinking to do.

When I finally emerged from the garden, the first three servants I met bowed and told me Freda wanted to see me urgently in the throne room. I headed directly there and found everyone gathered before my throne — the Dires, Conner, Dad, and Freda. My sister hurried to my side.

"Where have you been?" she demanded. "We have been waiting for nearly an hour!"

"Waiting for what?" I asked blankly.

"Your betrothal ceremony, you great idiot!"

"What!" I stared at her. "Nobody told me!"

She glared. "I've had every servant in the castle looking for you for an hour. Where have you been hiding?"

"In the garden —"

"Never mind, never mind! Come on. We must finish the ceremony. And I do not want to hear any more nonsense about love or refusing to marry. It is your *duty*."

"Very well," I said.

Swallowing hard, I forced a smile. Best get it over with. I might marry Della Dire, but that didn't mean I had to see her in her true form. As long as she kept herself looking as beautifiul as she had in the rose garden, I could put up with her. It was, after all, for the good of Amber.

Freda took my arm and escorted me down a long, black carpet toward the others. I looked around the room. Servants had been busy redecorating in my absense. In addition to the black carpet, new tapestries covered the walls, their patterns constantly moving in a way that made my skin crawl. I would have torn them all down and burned them, but they had to be here for a reason.

"Why change the room?" I asked softly.

"It is tradition," she murmured. "We may be exiles from the Courts of Chaos, but that does not mean we should forget our heritage. And remember — you do this not for yourself, but for your family. You *must* go through with the ceremony."

I nodded. "I understand."

The black carpet shifted underfoot like a living creature. The walls seemed to be bend in on me, and for a second, I wondered if another of the Feynim's creatures might be about to appear. No such luck, though — the spikard on my finger did nothing to warn me of danger; the bending seemed little more than an illusion created by the Chaos-items scattered throughout the room: the carpet, the wall-hangings, and more than anything else, Della Dire and her family.

The Dires stood in a clump. Della — at least, I assumed it was her under many layers of black, gauzy material — stood waiting between her parents.

"This is a union between two of the Great Houses," my father said. He raised a chalice into the air, lowered it, took a sip of whatever it contained. Then he passed it to Lord Dire, who echoed his words and also took a drink.

Dire passed the cup to me, and I accepted it. Then he produced a small knife, its handle made of dark stone carved with dragons swallowing their own tails.

"Our blood is our bond," he said. "Our families unite through you."

He slit his thumb and dribbled blood into the chalice for a second. The liquid inside began to bubble and froth. I glanced at my father, who gave a slight but encouraging nod. Dire passed the knife to him.

"Our blood is our bond," Dad repeated. He too slit his thumb and dribbled blood into the chalice. "Drink to the union of our families, son and daughter."

Freda whispered in my ear, "Annouce, 'Our families are joined' and drink."

"Our families are joined," I said in a flat voice. I raised the chalice to my lips and took a small sip.

It was a sweet wine, but I could still taste the blood in it. Freda nodded, smiling now.

"Give it to Della next," she whispered.

I offered the chalice to Della Dire.

She hesitated, then pushed it away.

"No," she said. The dark veils covering her face shifted for a second. Her beady little eyes stared straight at my brother.

Conner met her gaze, the corners of his lips turning up slightly.

Interesting. They knew each other?

"Drink!" Lord Dire thundered.

"I refuse," Della said.

"You *will* obey me!" he said in a voice that sent chills through me. He turned to me. "King Oberon — begin again."

"Our families are joined," I said a second time. I held out the chalice.

With the back of her hand, Della batted it away, slopping blood and wine across Freda and me. My sister gasped in outrage. I held my emotions carefully in check. Bursting out in happy song didn't seem the right reaction.

After the relief, though, a surprising rage flooded through me. Who was Della Dire to refuse *me*, the King of Amber? Was it better to be scorned by a woman I did not want to marry, or should I be insulted that I *was* being scorned?

Lord Dire roared his anger. My father turned his back and walked away silently. Freda stepped close to Della, slapped her hard across the face, then turned and followed Dad.

Shaking my head, I turned to Conner and found him trying to hide a smirk. Then he gave me a secret wink, and I knew he was responsible. Hadn't he promised to take care of the wedding for me?

"What is the meaning of this, Lord Dire?" I demanded, looking to my intended father-in-law.

Dire bowed stiffly from the waist. I did not move. Let me play the insulted party — who knew what benefits might be gained?

"My apologies, Oberon," he said in a strained voice. "My daughter is strong-willed. It will be beaten out of her before daybreak tomorrow, at which time the ceremony may continue without interruption."

I raised one hand.

"Della has made her feelings abundantly clear, Lord Dire. The fault is not yours. It is best to put off the ceremony, perhaps permanently. An unhappy union is not in anyone's best interest. I bid you a safe journey home to the Courts of Chaos."

Turning, head held high, I stalked away. Conner fell in step behind me.

Outside the door, I paused long enough to glance back. Lord Dire was dragging his daughter — now sobbing — from the room. The rest of his retinue trailed, grim-faced.

"So much for my wedding," I said to Conner. Things could not have gone better. And yet I felt a strange twinge of disappointment. Della Dire had been quite beautiful in the garden. I hoped I hadn't made a mistake.

"I told you I'd take care of it."

"Yes, but I didn't believe you!"

"Don't worry." He patted my shoulder with mock sympathy. "Freda will find you another bride!"

Ten minutes later, the two of us sat alone in the my bedroom, a bottle of wine at hand. I raised my cup to him in salute.

"A job well done!" I said.

"Thank you!"

"Now —" I drank deeply and settled back, studying him over the rim of my cup. "Tell me what you did."

"Oh . . . I simply offered her an alternative."

I nodded, my suspicions growing as I remembered the look Della had given him.

"She's in love with you, isn't she?" I asked.

He shrugged modestly. "Our father isn't the only one who knows how to romance a lady of Chaos, you know. A few soft words, a few love-poems . . . Della wanted love, not marriage. I offered it to her." He suddenly grinned. "Feel free to take notes, little brother."

I laughed. "If she's your girlfriend now, you're welcome to her!" Better him than me. "I have larger problems to deal with. Did Freda tell you about Aber?"

His lips tightened, and he gave a curt nod. "We must find a way to kill him before he does anything."

"Exactly. Ready to go hunting?"

"What — now?"

"Do you have something you'd rather do?"

"Almost anything. But go ahead. I'll watch your back."

Rising, he came around to stand beside me.

I drew Aber's new Trump from my pouch and raised it to eye level. Almost immediately, the colors grew vibrant and a figure — distant, wavering — appeared.

NINETEEN

t was my brother Aber, though I had a hard time focusing on him. His image kept shifting and jumping. He had to be very far away . . . in a distant Shadow, perhaps, or even the Courts of Chaos. I knew I was lucky to be able to contact him at all.

And he had changed. Just like the image on the Trump I still held, the left side of his face now sagged as though he had suffered a stroke, and his skin had an unwholesome yellowish tinge. The stiff high collar of his pearl-embroidered blue shirt hid the place where I had cut off his head so many years ago. He must have quite a scar from that particular wound.

"Who —" he began, and I noticed his voice had changed. It had grown lower and gravelly. He stopped, squinting. He seemed to be having as much trouble seeing me as I had seeing him.

My gaze drifted to the chamber behind him. Maybe I could find a clue as to his location from the objects in the room. Unfortunately, they all wavered like he did, blurry and half-recognizable.

Slowly, as I continued to concentrate on it, the room became clearer . . . it was a artist's workshop, but dark and shadowy. Oil paintings in various stages of completion lined the walls, some portraits, some showing weird landscapes that seemed to move and shift as my gaze settled on them. Sketches and pencil studies lay everywhere.

Non of it surprised me; Aber had been — and probably still was — quite a talented artist. He had made most of the Trumps I had lost in the sea.

"You —" he breathed, and I realized he could now see me as clearly as I saw him. His voice dripped with hatred and resentment.

"I see you've kept busy, brother," I said. I folded my arms and smiled. Let him think I had forgotten or forgiven his betrayal. It might put him off guard — and give me a chance to finish the job properly this time.

He smoothed his voice. "You found Isadora's missing Trumps, I see. She told me she'd lost them. Shall I assume you have no intention of giving them back?"

"They are mine now."

"Okay." He shrugged. "I can always make more."

"You look well, for a dead man."

"A murdered man never rests easy."

"I'm used to the dead staying dead."

"Don't think you can get away with murdering family members. Isadora has sworn to avenge me."

"I *was* a little confused as to the reason for her attack," I admitted.

"You killed her favorite brother." He smiled pointedly. "Isn't that reason enough?"

Beside me, Conner broke in with a laugh.

"Favorite Brother — meaning *you*?" he said. "Isadora hates you! The last time I heard her mention your name, she compared you to a dung-beetle! Locke was always her favorite."

"Locke," he said, "is dead."

"So are you," I pointed out. Maybe we could find out more by keeping him off balance.

Aber's smile mocked me. "Come back to the Courts, both of you. You'll see how well Isadora and I get along now. We have a lot in common now. She has become . . . quite devoted to me."

So, they were in the Courts of Chaos . . . and that meant Aber must still have King Swayvil's support — or perhaps his sufferance. Could the King of Chaos be the one who had brought him back from the dead? Or had it been Isadora, through some twisted sense of family loyalty?

Conner started to reply, but I held up my hand. He yielded to me.

"I destroyed the creature you sent," I told Aber. "If you try anything like that again, I'll do more than chop off your head."

A look of puzzlement crossed his face long enough to tell me he hadn't sent the shadow-creature and didn't know what I was talking about — but he covered it up with a shrug and another lopsided grin. If I had any lingering doubts, they vanished. This *was* my dead brother. I knew it.

"I do have one new trick," he said. "Let me show it to you."

I stretched out my hand. "Sure. Come through and we'll talk. I've done a lot of thinking over the last three years. When I killed you, I acted in haste. I'd still like to hear your side of things. Maybe it's not too late . . . maybe we can still work things out." Or maybe I can kill you again.

"Feeling nervous, Oberon?" The mocking tone returned. "Afraid

Isadora will finish the job next time?"

I laughed. "I don't think you heard the real story of our fight. Isadora attacked me from behind and in the dark. I was unprepared and unarmed. She still lost. As a warrior, she's a blundering amateur." I stuck out my hand again. "Come on, Aber. Let's talk. If you weren't family, I wouldn't give you a second chance."

"Better if you come here," he said smoothly. "I would feel much, ah, *safer*."

I shook my head. We knew each other too well. Between Isadora's sword and Aber's skill with magic, I'd never get out alive.

"Another time," I said.

"As you wish. I'll show you my trick anyway. Watch this!"

He raised his hand, made a curious gesture — and suddenly the Trump I was holding burst into flames.

I dropped the card with a surprised yelp as mocking laughter sounded all around.

TWENTY

hat hurt, damn you!" I shouted, blowing on scorched fingers. A faint curl of smoke lingered in the air.

The card landed face-down on the carpet. Our connection had been severed; Aber couldn't see or hear me anymore. And I didn't think he'd bother to answer if I tried to contact him again with another Trump.

As I continued to blow on my fingers, I consoled myself with one fact: at least I knew my brother really *was* alive. And he must be on good terms with King Swayvil to be living in the Courts of Chaos again. What had he promised the king — my head on a platter? That might well explain Isadora's sudden interest in killing me.

"Quite a trick," Conner said. Bending, he retrieved the Trump and examined it carefully. "No damage. I wonder how he did it?"

"I don't know, and I don't care. He's *alive*! Aber's *alive*!"

Conner shrugged. "So what? Forget him. We have a lot more to worry about right now — like Isadora. If she's trying to kill you, you're a dead man!"

I made a gesture of dismissal. "I doubt she'll be back. She lost our first fight, remember. There's no reason for her to risk another attack. For all she knows, I'll kill her the next time."

"You're fooling yourself. All you've done is make her mad, and she's even more dangerous that way. She's a *much* bigger threat than Aber. She's better with a sword than anyone else in our family. She's fought hundreds of duels in the Courts. She'll kill you easily, and she'll do it without a second's thought!"

"You're forgetting one thing — she has no reason to be after me."

"What do you mean? Aber said —"

"Aber lied, like always!" I grimaced. "Nothing he tells us can be taken at face value. She wanted to avenge his death? Not likely!"

"Why not?"

"Well, for starters . . . he's not dead, is he?"

He paused. "Not anymore."

"Then why bother to avenge him? What exactly is there *to* avenge?"

"You have a point," he admitted slowly. "But even so . . ."

"We're missing something," I said, trying to work through the details. "Her attack doesn't make any sense, and it ought to. Every event is caused by something else. If you follow that chain of events to its root — to the original cause — it should all become clear."

"Then what's the root cause? Aber's death?"

"No. I wish I knew where Isadora's been for the last three years. That might explain a lot."

Conner nodded. "She just vanished from Juniper . . ."

"She went off to find help against Swayvil, remember. So where *was* she? In the Courts of Chaos? One of its Shadows . . . perhaps the Beyond?"

"I don't think so. We were all there. Someone would have mentioned her if she had returned, too." He paused a moment, thinking.

"What are the other possibilities?" I said. "Captured by Swayvil?"

"Wouldn't she be dead?" he said. "Swayvil killed everyone else he took."

"Perhaps. He got Aber to work for him, though. Why not Isadora?"

"She wouldn't agree to work against our family."

Slowly I paced, trying to recall everything I had ever heard about my sister. The real problem was, I simply didn't know her — or very much about her. But I did know she had no reason to try to kill me.

I paused long enough to grab a decanter of whiskey from the cart by the wall. Pulling the stopper, I took a long drink. When I offered him the bottle, though, Conner laughed and shook his head.

"Too early for me," he said.

I snorted and took another long swallow. It wasn't too early for *me*. Not with more crazed family members trying to finish me off.

Then a horrible thought struck.

"What if," I said, "Isadora went to the Feynim for help?"

Conner sucked in a startled breath. "She wouldn't!"

"Why not? She's a great warrior; she wouldn't fear them. They are a natural choice for allies. They defeated Chaos once. Why not again?"

"That's only a theory," he said, "and not a very good one. I want proof. You don't have any."

"No. Not yet, anyway."

"Here's a simpler explanation. Aber has been telling her nothing but lies about us for the last three years. He's poisoned her against us. Maybe, once she learns the truth, she'll decide to join us here. We could certainly use her talents."

I shook my head. "No. I don't believe it's that simple. You said she hated Aber. Why would she listen to his lies to begin with?"

He chewed his lip thoughtfully. "Good point."

"Exactly!" I took another gulp of whiskey. "If Isadora believes she's a better fighter than me, she wouldn't try to stab me in the back. She'd ride up to the Castle Amber, challenge me to a duel, and carve me into scraps of dogmeat."

"How do you know?"

"Because that's what *I* would have done in her place. It makes a lasting impression on your enemies. Half the work of being a great warrior is getting people to believe in your reputation."

"I guess."

I began to pace again. I needed to look at everything differently. Instead of the motive, I needed to examine the attack itself. Dad had always said you could learn a lot from your enemies if you looked at their plans and strategies.

Mentally, I replayed the attack. Isadora came after me in the dark and from behind, while I was alone and unarmed. That was hardly an honorable approach to combat. Nor was it something I would have expected from a warrior who took pride in her craft.

And that meant . . . what? That it hadn't been her plan? Could the Feynim have sent her? Or . . .

"Aber," I said suddenly. The whole attack reeked of him. It had been *sneaky*. Who else would go after me in the dark and from behind?

"What do you mean?" Conner asked. "Aber hurt her?"

"No . . . he's controlling her, somehow. It has to be a spell or a charm of some kind. I don't know! *Something* magical. I don't believe

Isadora would attack me unless he made her do it."

"Hmm."

"Think about it," I continued. "Aber must have planned that ambush, not Isadora. She wouldn't stab me in the back, would she?"

"I wouldn't have thought so." His brow furrowed. "That part didn't sound like her. But I *can* see Aber doing it!"

I nodded. "Exactly."

"It *does* make a certain amount of sense," he admitted. "But if Aber has some kind of a magical hold over her, how can we break it? We don't even know what it is!"

"Freda can do it," I said with more certainty than I felt. "She'd enjoy figuring out how to unravel Aber's spells. Dad, too, for that matter."

"Given time, they can probably do it." He frowned. "But what if you're wrong? What if she wants you dead because . . . I don't know . . . you didn't manage to save Locke in Juniper? Or maybe she hates the new Shadows and wants them gone?"

"She was with us in Juniper. She knows how Locke died." Our brother had fallen fighting hell-creatures sent by Swayvil before he seized the throne of Chaos. "I couldn't have saved him if I'd done anything differently."

"That was just an example. She could have some other motive. Or maybe she just plain doesn't like *you!*"

"Then I'll have to be more charming the next time we meet." I almost laughed. How could she not like *me*? Impossible!

"Okay, okay." He sighed and shook his head. "I guess it's a pretty good plan. Now we just have to find a way to get Isadora away from him. The hard part will be taking her alive."

"We'll be subtle. Someone here must have a Trump for her. Maybe Freda — why are you grinning like that?"

"I have her Trump," he said. "I've had it for years."

"Good! Then you can use it to lure her here. Tell her . . . tell her you hate me, too, and you want her help to kill me. That should bring her running."

"I'll try," he said. "She always liked me. Maybe she'll trust me this time. Hopefully she won't try to kill me, too!"

"I can watch your back."

"No, I'd rather you didn't. I need her to trust me, and that means I have to speak to her openly and honestly. If she sees you, she'll know it's a trap. Not only is she the greatest warrior in our family, she's got a paranoid streak even worse than Dad's."

"Who doesn't these days?" I nodded slowly; it *did* sound like a good plan, though. "How does she feel about Freda? Maybe you could both talk to her . . ."

He shrugged. "I don't think Isadora ever gave Freda much thought. I once overheard her say that all the women in our family were weak and foolish creatures, spending all their time on magic, beauty-potions, and intrigue rather than anything useful, like weapons."

"Too bad she's my sister. Otherwise I think I'd have to marry her!"

Conner groaned. "Oh no . . . think of your poor children!"

"All right." I nodded slowly. "Contact Isadora in private. But I'm going to be in the next room, with a drawn sword just in case. And . . .

be careful. I don't want to lose you. "

"I don't want to lose myself, either!" He hesitated. "You have that look again . . . what are you thinking?"

"What look?"

"Like you're going to do something crazy."

"Yes?" I smiled slowly. A vague plan *had* been forming in the back of my mind. I didn't quite have it down yet, but if it worked, it might well solve many of my problems. If only Aber would cooperate . . .

I changed the subject. We still had time enough for my plans once we had Isadora.

"Call her now," I said.

"Right now? From here?"

"Yes. I'll wait outside."

"All right." He reached into the air and plucked a Trump from nothingness: he had used the power of the Logrus to fetch it. I saw Isadora's figure drawn upon the front. She held a sword that slowly dripped blood . . . probably Aber's idea of humor.

"Remember, I'll be outside," I said, drawing my sword. "If you need me, just shout."

He nodded. "Right."

I closed the door and stood waiting. I strained to hear, but no sounds reached me. How long would this take? After five minutes, though, nothing had happened.

Opening the door a crack, I peeked in. Conner stood in the middle of the room, staring hard at the Trump. But nothing seemed to be happening. At last he lowered it.

"Can't reach her?" I asked, coming inside again.

He shook his head. "No. But that could mean anything. She could be too far, or asleep, or . . . I don't know. Preoccupied."

I sighed. "Well, at least we tried. We can deal with her when the time comes. Right now, we have a more pressing worry."

And I proceeded to tell him about my afternoon trip to see Queen Moins and her kingdom under the sea . . . and how it contained an inverse image of the Pattern.

"Did you try walking this version of the Pattern?" he asked.

I frowned. "No. It never occurred to me."

"What would happen if you did?"

And interesting thought. *Was* it similar enough to the real Pattern to work the same way? Would it allow me to transport myself anywhere I wanted to go?

Suddenly I wanted to find out. But I couldn't very well go alone. Time for another trip to Caer Beatha . . .

"Up for a midnight swim?" I asked.

"With those mermaid friends of yours?" He chuckled and shook his head. "What would Della say if she caught me frolicking at night with mermaids?"

"They aren't mermaids. They don't have tails." I grinned. "Besides, the Dires have probably left Amber already. Lord Dire was pretty upset."

"I *had* hoped to get to know Della better . . . once you were out of the way, of course."

I gave him a wicked grin. "For your sake, I hope she's gone! There will be time enough for romance later."

"Okay. When do we go? Tonight?"

"Yes. We'll go before dinner and see if we can find them."

"Better yet, we'll bring dinner!" he said. "We'll have Cook do it properly."

"And wine!" I added. "Lots of wine!"

We grinned at each other. Our little expedition this evening suddenly sounded like a lot of fun.

TWENTY-ONE

t takes a lot to keep a secret in a castle. Between the cooks who prepared our light picnic supper, the valets who packed up towels, blankets, and changes of clothing, and the stable-master who readied our horses, half the castle must have known of our expedition.

Sure enough, Freda showed up just as we were mounting up for the ride to the beach. I sat astride Apollo, my usual black stallion, who had returned to the castle without me the night before, and Conner had his bay gelding.

"You cannot leave," Freda told me, walking up beside me. She grabbed the halter and pulled Apollo to a stop.

"Why ever not?" I demanded.

"Because of our guests! You are still their host. You abandoned us at dinner last night. But to skip another meal? Intolerable!"

"Don't tell me the Dires are still here!" I frowned. "Why haven't they left?"

"Why should they? I have worked everything out with Lord and Lady Dire. Tomorrow, we will have another betrothal ceremony, and —"

"No," I said bluntly. It had become a point of honor. "I have been insulted. I *cannot* marry her now."

She sighed. "Oberon . . ."

"Do you know whom she wants to marry?" I asked

"You, of course!"

"Conner."

I said it so bluntly, it caught her off guard. She looked entirely at a loss for words. For a long time, she just looked at our brother, who grinned back at her.

"Is this true?" she finally asked in an odd voice.

"Well . . . we have exchanged a few love notes," he admitted.

I added, "Poems, too, I hear."

Freda made little strangling noises.

"Lady Dire makes my skin crawl, and Della Dire isn't much better. Better to stick the whole lot of them with someone else. No offense," I said to Conner. After all, Della seemed to appeal to him.

"None taken," he said with a laugh. "I know she's beautiful, and I know I'm lucky to have her. You were a fool to throw all that away!"

Freda said in exasperation, "You have ruined everything, the pair of you. How could you . . . what can I . . ." She broke off. "Perhaps things can still be salvaged. At the very least, you must invite Lord Dire to accompany you. It is only polite to share your sport."

Sport? If she thought Conner and I were off to go hunting, let her! The fewer people who knew about Braëyis, Queen Moins, and Caer Baetha, the better off we would be.

"Do you think he'd want to join us?" I asked.

"Yes," she said, smiling hopefully. "He likes you."

"Then no," I said flatly. I might have considered inviting him if I'd known he would refuse.

"Freda," said Conner, "I agree with Oberon. The Dires are better off here, entertained by you and Dad in the style you all enjoy."

Freda scowled at him. "Be quiet. You are not helping. Besides, the decision is Oberon's, not yours."

"Oberon?" he said, turning to me.

I spread my hands helplessly. "Sorry, Freda. Our plans are set. Don't worry, we'll be back well before dawn – in time, I'm sure, to have breakfast with the Dires if they're still around. They must realize our lives don't stop just because they're visiting."

When I nudged Apollo with my knees and heels, he pulled free from Freda, burst into a canter, and shot through the castle gates.

"Oberon!" she called. "You will regret this!"

I did not look back. I actually felt *free*. Free from the duties and obligations which had so weighed me down. Free from the marriage I didn't want. Free to go off and truly enjoy myself for the first time since . . . since I didn't know when!

Once out of the castle, we let our horses pick their own pace and simply enjoyed the ride. The sun shone brilliantly overhead, and a pleasant breeze gusted, relieving the heat of the afternoon. Like brothers do, we chatted about inconsequential things . . . tales of past campaigns, loves and losses, the best and the worst of our experiences.

Conner had really come into his own in the last few years. It was a pleasure to talk about military matters again, instead of architecture, politics, or magic. Conner demonstrated a keen insight into how best to make use of the strengths of our men. I wished I had known him longer. I would have liked him at my side in Ilerium. We would have had such fun in those days. . . .

It was dinner-time when we finally neared the beach. With the sun just beginning to settle into the west, a light wind at our backs, and adventure ahead, I could not have asked for a more perfect day. I felt buoyed up with optimism.

And why not? I had escaped Della Dire's clutches. Aber's plot had been thwarted, Isadora had been driven off, and I hadn't heard a peep from the Feynim since I had killed their creature. Best of all, a night of pleasure lay ahead. I could relax for the moment and simply enjoy myself.

The road narrowed to a track and wound between sand dunes toward the beach. A strong, moist wind came off the water here, carrying the sharp smell of brine. I smiled to myself, remembering Braëyis. It would be good to see her again. And I looked forward to introducing Conner to her friends!

As we topped the final dune and the sea came into view, my ring pulsed in warning. I reigned in Apollo and drew my sword, looking around fast.

"What's wrong?" Conner demanded, pulling up beside me. He also drew his sword.

"I don't know," I said, standing up in my stirrups to see better. What had the spikard sensed?

Conner twisted in his saddle. "I don't see anything —"

A strange warbling cry sounded from somewhere to our left. Then, in response, more than a dozen men leaped out of the dunes around us. Sand streamed off their cloaks; they had been buried just below the surface. Some held pikes; others held swords. Screaming savagely, they rushed straight at us.

"So much for our picnic," Conner grumbled. "Next time, I'm going to listen to Freda."

"We'll eat after the fight," I said, kicking Apollo forward. "Ride through them!"

Snorting angrily, my stallion lunged ahead, then reared as men blocked our path. Hooves flailing, he struck out. He knocked their leader to the ground, then trampled him. The man died with a gurgling shriek of pain.

All the attackers seemed to be converging on me. Luckily Conner had my left side. I couldn't be taken from behind while I fought them off to the right.

Apollo spotted an opening and plunged forward. Conner followed. As we raced through their midst, I hacked and slashed like a demon. With a backhanded swing, I cut one man nearly in half, then rounded and knocked the sword flying from a second man's grasp. He leaped clear of my darting blade, sprawling backward and rolling to safety, but without a weapon he posed little threat. The others began to break and flee. I gave chase, and Apollo responded to my knee-press commands like the warhorse he was, biting and kicking and doing as much damage as he could. We were both soaked with blood in five minutes.

Our few remaining attackers regrouped and tried to close on me, but they seemed to be losing their enthusiasm. The pikemen wielded their weapons with too much caution, as if they weren't truly familiar with them. That, or lying hidden in the sand for hours had made them tired and clumsy.

Laughing, my blade dripping with gore, I took a wild pleasure in the slaughter. I severed a pikeman's hand and left him gaping helplessly at the stump. Then I slashed another man's face and chest so the skin peeled and flapped like a banner. He dropped his weapon and tried to press his face back into position as blood streamed over his hands. Lady Dire would have loved the gush of blood. He slid to his knees a second later, then fell and didn't move.

Screaming a battle-cry, I rushed at all the remaing half dozen. They dropped their weapons and fled in all directions.

I chose one man, rode him down, and then Apollo carried me past.

"Conner?" I called.

"Right behind you!" he shouted back.

I galloped twenty yards up the beach, turned for another pass. Conner, laughing madly, sprays of blood coloring his face and shirt crimson, seemed to have enjoyed the fight as much as I had. Truly we were men destined for action!

"Are you all right?" I called, reining back Apollo. We weren't done with the other attackers yet. They had disappeared over the sand dune . . . possibly three or four survivors from the fifteen or so who had ambushed us.

"Come on!" he cried. "We'll finish them!"

"Leave at least one alive. I want answers."

"Sure!" He grinned. "We can try out the new dungeons. We haven't had any prisoners to interrogate yet. Dad had the carpenters build a rack and a pair of iron maidens during the storm."

I shrugged. "I've never really enjoyed torture."

"Since when does pleasure have anything to do with it?"

"True." If they had information I wanted, I'd get it out of them by any means necessary.

Still on horseback, we started for the dune at a trot. Unless they had a Trump, our attackers wouldn't be getting away anytime soon.

"Of course," he said, "if you're feeling squeamish, you can start off with small stuff. Dad has a pretty good collection of thumb-screws and hand-crackers."

Halfway back to the dune where we had been ambushed, the spikard on my finger pulsed again. I frowned, but pulled Apollo to a halt.

"Wait!" I said.

"What is it?" Conner demanded.

"There's danger ahead." Another ambush? Or something else . . . something magical?

"How do you know?"

"Don't worry about it. I just do."

I had never told him my ring had the power to warn me of dangers it sensed. Since Aber's betrayal, I had been keeping a lot to myself.

I ran through the fight in my mind. Conner had killed at least two and probably three. I had gotten eight. That left . . . four or five?

But that number did not include whoever gave the signal to attack. Aber? No, it couldn't be him — taking part in am ambush wasn't his style. He would have sent a lieutenant.

Isadora!

At that moment, a woman in silver armor came over the closest dune, her long blond hair blowing freely in the wind. Conner sucked in his breath.

Isadora had been behind the attack. Apparently she'd been in Amber long enough this time to get over her dizziness. She looked grimly determined to finish the job she'd started.

Giving a long, warbling wolf-howl of a war cry, she charged straight at me. She had a sword in each hand.

"Get the others," I said to Conner. "I'll take care of Isadora."

"Better to run," he said. "She'll cut you to pieces."

"I've already beaten her once. I can do it again. Besides, in case she *isn't* under Aber's control, I have to give her a chance to talk things out with me. Maybe I can reason with her."

Nudging Apollo to a trot, I rode forward to meet her. I held my sword up.

"Talk first!" I called.

She drew to a halt, staring at me suspiciously. Obviously I was up to some sort of trick. What must Aber have told her about me?

"Why do you keep attacking me?" I demanded. "What have I ever done to you?"

"I know everything you've done!" she snarled.

"For example?"

"You weakened Chaos. You created these damn Shadow-worlds. You got half of our family killed — and you murdered Aber!"

"Not true, mostly," I said. "Dad created the Pattern and the Shadows, not me. I did kill Aber . . . but he deserved it for betraying me."

"I'll see your blood for it!"

"I don't suppose you'd care to hear my side of it first?"

"No!"

"Very well. I never put off the inevitable. If you want to fight — so be it. We'll finish it now!"

I swung down from the saddle and faced her. She stuck one sword in the sand beside her, then took up a classic duelist's stance, the tip of her sword pointed at my face.

Slowly we circled each other, but I held back on my attack.

"Did you ever stop to think that your actions don't make sense?" I asked. "You hate Aber. You always have. Why help him now?"

She feinted, then lunged. I parried easily.

"I'll fight you," I continued, "but I think Aber has you under a spell. You aren't responsible for your actions. *Think*, Isadora! Remember how you feel about Aber!"

She didn't bother to reply. She lunged again, and again I parried, sword ringing on sword. She was testing my speed and skill. Apparently I hadn't impressed her much; an almost mocking smile flitted across her face, as if she expected to dispatch me quickly and easily.

Her next attack came with blinding speed, sure footwork, and unconventional sequences of thrusts and counters. That whistling blade probed my every defense, moving with an amazing speed. I could barely cover myself as I retreated. Gods, was she fast!

One of the differences between a duel and a battlefield fight is that it doesn't hurt to surrender territory when you only have one opponent. I yielded fast before her onslaught. Now I saw why everyone thought of her as the best fighter in our family. Her skill with a blade dazzled me. I'd never come up against anyone quite like her before. Had I been a happy spectator instead of the target of her fury, I would have marveled at her technique. *This* is how duels were supposed to be fought!

It took all my effort to hold her off. Her stamina was incredible, too. As the minutes passed, cold sweat began to trickle down my face and back and armpits. My heart thundered in my chest, while she barely seemed winded.

Worst of all, she seldom left room for a counter-attack. The few openings I found and probed met with swift and immediate ripost. Again and again she drove me backward. Whenever I did manage to take the offensive for a minute, I unexpectedly found our positions reversed and her in control once more.

I switched from right to left hand with my sword. She did the same. Our blades rang as loudly as before when we closed. She threw me back ten feet, then rushed in with a series of savage downward blows that would have crushed a lesser man's defenses.

This time I parried two-handed, putting all my muscle into the swings. If nothing else, I had her in sheer physical strength. If only I could break her grip and send her sword flying, the match would be over. But somehow — though my ringing parries must have numbed her arm from fingertips to shoulder — she kept her grip on the hilt and even managed a back-handed slash that would have laid my chest open if I hadn't leaped back in time.

Panting, glaring at each other, we circled again. She switched back to a right-handed grip. Sweat finally began to trickle down her face, plastering her hair to her forehead. Clearly I wasn't the easy target she'd expected. Maybe I could use that to my advantage.

"We can still call it a draw," I said in even tones, trying to sound reassuring and in control. "We can still go back to Amber and talk things over with Dad and Freda. I don't want to kill you. You're my sister — I know Aber has a spell working on your mind."

"Shut up!"

"No. You need to know you're mistaken — about Aber and everything else. He's put some sort of a charm on you. Think about it, Isadora. Have you ever liked him?"

"Shut up and *die!*"

She rushed me, sword swinging, and once more we came together with a series of nerve-shattering blows.

The next time we broke apart, sweating and gasping for breath, I took a moment to ask the question that had been bothering me for so long.

"Tell me," I said, "why you're doing this for Aber. You hate him. Conner told me about it. Remember the time he had your favorite horse stuffed and mounted as a trophy?"

This time she did not bother to reply, but launched straight into another series of half-crazed blows that forced me to the edge of the sea. The tip of her sword hummed and flew like an angry wasp. As waves splashed across my boots, I realized I'd backed up too far.

She thought she had me now, and she pressed harder than ever. Her techniques still showed a perfect sense of timing and balance. She easily could have been the best opponent I had ever fought.

Thrust. Parry — parry —

The universe narrowed down to her eyes and the whistling tip of her sword. I felt a cold sweat drenching my whole body.

Parry — parry — parry —

Minutes dragged out. Did she never tire? I felt the first signs of muscle fatigue, a slight burning across my back and shoulders. If I lived through this fight, I would have to double my workouts; clearly I wasn't in as good a shape as I had thought.

Thrust – thrust – parry –

A duel is different from a battlefield fight in other ways besides your ability to retreat. There is no moving tide of men and horses around you, no war-cries or death-screams or clashes of steel-on-steel to distract you from your opponent. Everything comes down to the quickness of your blade, the steadiness of your arm, and the sureness of your footwork. And, all other things being equal, your strength and stamina. If you couldn't gain an advantage any other way, you tried to wear down your opponent.

Unfortunately, I felt outclassed by Isadora. Only by the barest whisker of speed and luck did I manage to hold my own.

The ring on my finger must have sensed my difficulties. On some of her moves, it began to signal to me, reading her intent. One quick pulse meant a feint. Two meant a double feint. Nothing meant a direct attack.

I felt myself weakening, even if I didn't yet show it in my swordplay. I would have to end the fight, and soon, before she took advantage of a too-slow parry.

I began to time her moves, waiting for my chance. My ring pulsed twice – a double-feint. *Now!*

Ignoring her blade, ignoring all logic, I closed with her. With the hilt of my sword, I punched her in the head. The blow would have staggered any normal person, but Isadora barely flinched. I saw that my thumb had gouged her temple. Blood ran freely down into her right eye.

"Yield!" I commanded. "That's first blood!"

I saw the slight downturn of her mouth, as if she suddenly began to doubt herself.

And the blood had already begun to affect her vision. Unexpectedly she disengaged and retreated, wiping at her forehead with the back of her free hand. If anything, that opened the wound further.

"Yield," I said strongly, advancing on her. "Throw down your sword. This doesn't have to end in your death."

"No!" She glared, the pure hatred in her eyes telling me more clearly than words that she would never give up. Whatever our brother had done to control her, it left no room for common sense.

I might be able to turn that to my advantage, though. After all, she hadn't been able to touch me yet. She had to be wondering, could I be the better swordsman?

"You can't fight with that wound," I announced in a light voice, as if I had known I would win all the time. I lowered my blade slightly, as if I had nothing more to fear from her. That ought to infuriate her more than anything else. "I will spare your life, sister. I am always generous in victory."

It worked. Her eyes narrowed to slits and her jaw tightened.

"Mere luck!" she snarled.

"You're welcome to think so." I gave a chuckle. "But this is twice now you've lost to me. Do we have to make it three times for you to give up?"

"The fight isn't over!"

"Yes, it is. And you've lost, Isadora. Your hands are slick with blood and sweat. You can barely see. Face the truth! It's over!"

She did not reply, but instead rushed me, warbling her battle-cry. I parried and slashed, and this time *she* was the one who barely leaped back in time. The tip of my sword rang off the steel of her breastplate.

Still chuckling softly, I stalked forward. Her eyes flicked uncertainly from my face to the tip of my sword, and she began to retreat.

I had her! I knew it then. Her spirit had broken. Though she might fight on, she no longer believed she could win.

"So much for the greatest fighter in our family!" I called mockingly. "Too prideful to use her head in battle. Too dumb to yield when a fight is lost. Better to keep backing up until I get tired of chasing you. Yield, Isadora!"

"*I – never – yield!*" she gasped, and she lowered her sword and rushed me.

Giving full voice to my own battle-cry, I leaped to engage her. I used both hands on my sword, parrying increasingly wild and frantic swings.

Then I seized the initiative and hammered at her. Our swords screamed and threw sparks as they struck. Again and again I pounded at her defenses, without hesitation, without mercy, without pause.

I drove her back up the beach, then up a dune, to where the seagrass began. Blood and sweat still streamed down her face and into her eyes, half blinding her. She barely managed to keep my sword at bay. I felt her weakening, and it gave me new strength.

Then I smashed my blade across hers. With a dull *crack!* her sword shattered. The hilt tumbled from her suddenly nerveless fingers, and she gasped in pain.

The tip of my blade hovered an inch from her throat. I paused.

"Yield!" I commanded. "I will not give you another chance!"

"No!" she cried, tears streaming down her cheeks. "No!" She grabbed at her belt and tried to draw a knife.

By all rights, I should have killed her. It would have simplified my life. Instead, I swung the flat of my blade and struck the left side of the head. She went down silently, eyes flat and glassy.

Panting, drenched in sweat, I dropped to my knees beside her. The sword tumbled from my hand. I had never felt so exhausted after a battle.

Without a doubt, she had been the greatest warrior I had ever faced — far better than our father, far better than any soldier of Chaos I had met. And this time I had won honestly . . . or nearly so. The spikard *had* helped turn the fight in my favor.

"Thanks," I told it.

At least it had been Isadora's sword rather than mine which broke. Yet another reason I needed *King-maker* . . .

Slowly I looked around for Conner. It had been growing dark, I discovered; I had been so caught up in the fight that I hadn't noticed. We must have been in combat for at least an hour — and maybe longer.

So where had my brother gone? And what of Isadora's men? He must have accounted for all of them, since no one else was trying to kill me at the moment.

"Conner!" I shouted.

"Over here!" a distant voice called. I turned, then spotted him sitting atop a sand dune about a hundred feet away. He sat slumped with his back to a scraggly little bush. In the growing darkness, I hadn't picked out his form.

Taking a deep breath, I picked up my sword and forced myself to my feet. Why hadn't Conner come over to check on me? Was he hurt?

I limped over to his side and flopped down beside him, still panting a bit. I really needed to work out more often. I had let my training go too much since becoming king of Amber.

"That was the most incredible fight I have ever seen," he said. "You were amazing."

"Thanks. How are you? Are you hurt?"

He looked terrible. So much blood covered his face and hands that I wondered if it could all be his. Even his clothing was soaked with it.

"I'm all right," he said with a half shrug. "Just a little tired and cut up, is all." He nodded toward our sister. "Is she —?"

"No, she's not dead." I gave a low chuckle. "She's just unconscious. She's too valuable to kill right now. There's a lot I want to learn from her."

"Like where to find Aber?"

"Yes . . . and maybe she has news of some of our other missing brothers and sisters. If she's still alive, there might be others, too."

"I hope so. Not knowing stinks." An expression of awe lingering on his face. "I still can't believe you won," he said. "No one in our family has *ever* beaten Isadora in a fight. Not even Locke. She was the best any of us had ever seen."

"Until now," I said.

"Yes . . . until now."

I shifted uncomfortably. This was too much praise for a simple soldier like me. I didn't want to get too full of myself; *I* knew I had barely held my own against her.

"Let's get you bandaged up," I said to change the subject. "Your head is seeping — there's blood dribbling down your cheek from that scalp wound. And I'd better check you over for broken bones."

"I'm all right. Nothing is broken."

"Let me be the judge of that." I had done more than my fair share of quick-and-dirty battlefield doctoring over the years, and despite all his assurances to the contrary, he looked a real mess.

I added, "After a battle, when the rush of combat is still upon you, it's easy to miss stuff. I've broken bones a dozen times in battles but not realized it till hours or even days later. Usually ribs or toes, but even so . . ."

Sighing, he gave in. "Fair enough."

"Lie back and give me your arm."

He did as instructed. I ran practiced hands across his arms, legs, shoulders, head, and chest, pressing the bones to see if anything moved where it shouldn't, probing each bloody or bruised area for actual damage. His head wound was the only real problem — a long, shallow slice across his forehead just above the hairline. It hung open, and I glimpsed the white of his flesh. It would have to be sewn up at Castle Amber; I couldn't do it here. He had gotten sand in it, too. It would have to be properly washed and dressed.

I'd leave that for the castle barber, who normally handled such things. Or maybe Freda, if Conner preferred her touch — she had a steady hand and a sure eye with needle and thread, as I knew from experience. She had sewed up my wounds at least half a dozen times since we'd come to Amber.

"Well?" he demanded.

"You'll *probably* live. Let me finish!"

I skinned back his eyelids and checked his pupils. In the last dying rays of daylight, they seemed normal enough, dilating then shrinking as I covered and uncovered them with the palm of my hand. He wasn't in shock.

"Okay, it's definite. You'll live." I sat back on my haunches. "You'll need stitches when we get home. Everything else is minor — nothing a big steak, a long soak in a hot tub, and a couple days' rest won't cure."

"Thanks. Now you can add 'Doc' to your other titles." He struggled to a sitting position, wincing sharply. "Ow!"

"Dizzy?" I asked.

"Yes!"

"Let it pass." He must be suffering from blood loss. Then I said, "Tell me what happened while I was fighting Isadora. Last I saw, you were rushing at six or seven men."

"It was seven," he said with a grin.

Modestly, he told how he had charged into the remaining soldiers' midst. They had attacked from both sides and managed to drag him from the saddle. Of course, he hadn't gone down easily — snapping one man's neck and breaking another's back in the process. On the ground, he snatched up a fallen sword and fought his way clear. Then he laid into the remaining three like a madman, showing no restraint and no mercy.

When he cut their leader in half from head to groin with a single blow, the last two fell to their knees and begged for their lives. And reluctantly, he held his sword.

"I saved them for questioning like you wanted," he finished, sounding a little grumpy about it.

"It was necessary." I looked around, but didn't spot the pair. "What did you do with them?"

"I left them back there." He nodded back toward the spot where we had been ambushed. "If only my thrice-damned horse hadn't gotten spooked and run off . . ."

"You *left them*?" I jolted upright. "What if they run away? Neither one of us is in any condition to track them down again —"

He gave a thoroughly wicked chuckle. "Don't worry about it — I cut their hamstrings. Did I forget to mention that part? They aren't going *anywhere* unless we carry or drag them."

I sank back. "And I thought *I* was the bloodthirsty one in the family!"

"We all have our vindictive sides . . . I don't like being dragged from my saddle."

I nodded. Two men to question . . . plus Isadora. Of course, we already knew Aber had sent them all. Between questioning the hirelings and freeing Isadora from whatever spell Aber had laid upon her, who knew what we might learn! Aber's present location . . . the names of any spies he'd already placed in Amber (and he had to have a few to know about our plans for a picnic tonight) . . . any future plans against me . . .

Conner said again, "Isadora . . . you had better go check on her. I still can't believe you *beat* her!"

"Of course I did!" I grinned as though it had been a sure thing all along. "Don't tell me you actually had doubts?"

He didn't answer, but I saw that once again I'd made another strong impression on him. *Good.* Let him tell everyone how I'd beaten Isadora *twice.* Perhaps, if enough people viewed me as the greatest fighter in the history of our family, our chances of being attacked would go down.

I climbed to my feet.

"I'll tie her up," I said, standing. "Can't have her disappearing, after all."

"I'll join you in a minute."

I nodded, then walked back to our sister. To my dismay, I found she had recovered consciousness enough to climb awkwardly to her hands and knees. Groaning, she spotted what remained of her sword. The hilt had a jagged six-inch piece of blade still attached . . . enough to make a nasty stabbing weapon.

She dove for it.

Not this time. I took two quick steps and struck the back of her head with the heavy pommel of my sword. Her skull gave a satisfying dull *thump,* then she collapsed face-down in the sand. I kicked the remains of her sword away, then rolled her onto her back to check her pulse. I couldn't have her dying on me, after all — not after what I'd gone through to take her alive!

TWENTY-TWO

ouching her throat, I found a slow but steady pulse. Like me, she had the constitution of an ox. She'd be back on her feet again soon if I didn't restrain her right now. I didn't want have to have to fight her again; next time, I might not be so lucky.

First, though, I rolled her onto her back and searched her clothing quickly and methodically . . . no point in tying her up if she could pull out some hidden blade and escape.

Sure enough, in addition to the pair of matched throwing knives in sheathes at her hip, I discovered a stiletto in her right boot and a garrote in her left boot. I also removed a deck of Trumps . . . not unexpected. I'd go through the cards at my leisure; there may be a few I'd want to add to my own deck.

Then I opened a small leather pouch and spilled out a handful of five-sided gold coins. Isadora's image had been stamped on the front of each. She must have set herself up as a queen or goddess in some distant Shadow.

She moaned again, and her eyes began to move rapidly beneath their lids. It wouldn't be much longer before she woke, and I couldn't have that . . . not yet, not until I was prepared for her.

I grabbed the garrote. It was a three-foot-long cord, braided from what looked like several dozen very thin metal wires. I tested it, but felt no give at all. It would certainly do to tie her hands.

With no consideration for any pain or discomfort I might cause, I trussed her up like a roasted chicken, cinching her hands and ankles behind her back. I even stuffed the empty coin-pouch in her mouth before gagging her with a strip torn from my own shirt. Lastly, I blind-folded her with another shirt-strip. If Aber or anyone else tried to contact her with a Trump, I didn't want her answering them.

Done, I sat back on my heels to consider the situation. Isadora wouldn't be escaping anytime soon — or so I hoped. If I couldn't keep her from trying to kill me now, I might as well give up.

Standing, I put two fingers to my lips and whistled sharply for Apollo. He came trotting over the top of a nearby sand dune, ears up, tail up, chewing happily on a mouthful of grass. He had been waiting patiently for me, as he had been trained to do.

"Good boy," I said, rubbing his nose. He sniffed for treats, but of course I didn't have anything now. Our pack-horse had vanished, tak-ing our food along for the ride. "Later," I promised him, "when we get back to the castle."

I heaved Isadora stomach-first across the saddle, then tied her in place with leather cords from the saddlebag. Not the most comfort-able position for a rider, but I found I really didn't care. As long as she wouldn't fall off and break her neck, it would do.

After that, I led Apollo over to Conner. My brother struggled to his feet unsteadily. Blood still trickled slowly down the side of his face; he looked pale and unsure of himself.

Suddenly Isadora began to make noises through the gag and

thrash about feebly. I hadn't left her much room to breathe, let alone escape.

I patted the back of her head softly, reassuringly. "Don't worry," I said in a gentle voice. "You aren't in any danger now. Dad and Freda will remove whatever spell you're under. Just be patient, sister."

That made her struggle all the more. Aber's magic had to be responsible; she didn't understand I was only trying to help.

Conner managed a sick grin. "I never thought I'd see the day Isadora wound up your prisoner," he said.

"It's better than the alternative."

"She wouldn't have taken *you* alive."

I paused. True, probably.

"Do you think you can walk all the way back to the castle?" I asked.

"Yes."

"You can sit in front of Isadora, if you want. Apollo won't mind the extra weight."

"I can make it." He shook his head gingerly. "I mostly had the wind knocked out of me, that's all. I'll be fine."

Spoken like a true soldier. He wouldn't admit to needing help even if he'd lost an arm and both legs.

He looked around. "Any sign of my horse?"

"I'll take a quick look for him. Here." I thrust Apollo's reins into his hands. That would give him something to hold onto. "Go ahead and start back. I'll catch up in a few minutes."

"What about those two men I left alive for you?"

I hesitated. In my concern over Isadora, I had forgotten about them.

"I'll send guards back to collect them," I said. "They aren't going anywhere. I don't think Aber will bother to rescue them."

"No, he won't."

Taking a deep breath, Conner turned toward the castle and set off across the dunes at a slow, stiff walk. His muscles had to be hurting. He hadn't been through nearly as many fights as I had, so he wouldn't have known what to expect.

If he thought he hurt now, just wait. Tomorrow would be ten times as bad. He thought I'd been joking about taking a long hot bath, but it would be the best thing to loosen up his muscles.

As I returned to the beach, the last of the sunset faded away in the west and the first stars of evening appeared overhead. Another hour and the moon would rise.

I walked up the beach, sand crunching under my boots, the hum of insects rising from the grass, looking for Conner's horse. Every few seconds I gave a loud whistle and called, "Hiero!" but the gelding didn't appear. For all I knew, he might have headed back to the castle on his own . . . or galloped ten miles up the beach in the other direction. In the dark, I couldn't see any hoofprints.

No sense wasting any more time searching for him. Shaking my head, I turned toward home. Considering how slowly Conner would be walking, it shouldn't take me long to catch up, even in the near darkness.

Then Queen Moins' song began. Once more that lilting, wordless, half-familiar tune rose from the sea floor, the notes tugging at something primal inside me.

Suddenly I *had* to go to her . . .

I *had* to hear the rest of that song!

Pausing, I gazed out across the now-glimmering sea. Dark figures appeared a hundred yards out, sliding with the ease of dolphins through the waves. Several beckoned, laughing, voices like bells. They remembered last night . . . they wanted me to join them again!

"Oberon . . ." a familiar voice called. It sounded like Braëyis. *"Oberon . . ."*

I ran into the wash, knee-deep. One of the dark figures swam toward me now with powerful strokes, then stood up in the shallows. Her skin glistened, slick and wet, and her long green-black hair lay plastered against her head. Lit from underneath by the water's glow, her eyes seemed impossibly huge and dark.

"Braëyis!" I said. I splashed out waist-deep to meet her. We kissed passionately for a long time, her arms cool and damp around my neck, her tongue hot against mine. Her fingers moved lower, and she began to fumble with my swordbelt. She wanted me to swim with her again tonight. *Expected* it.

Gently but firmly I returned her hands to my chest. "Not this time," I said. I hated to leave her behind, but what else could I do? I had to catch up with Conner, then take care of Isadora and the other two prisoners.

She tilted her head to one side and stared up into my eyes, puzzled. I knew this wasn't the answer she had expected. Yet I couldn't say what she most wanted to hear — not tonight, not with everything that had just happened.

"Do you hear the song?" she asked. "Queen Moins is singing it for *you*. It is *yours alone*."

"I know." And beautiful it was, rising and falling with the waves, tugging gently at my heart and my head. I found it hard to resist. More than anything, I *wanted* to join Braëyis in the water.

But I couldn't. Duty always comes before pleasure. That was the first rule every soldier learned.

"You must come!" she insisted. "Queen Moins says so! You will meet her again tonight!"

Once more her hands went to my belt. The music soared. The song commanded me, *summoned* me, before Queen Moins and her court.

But once again I shook my head. It simply could not happen. Not tonight.

"I'm sorry," I said.

"Oberon . . ." she whispered.

"Another time!" I planted a kiss on her forehead. "Queen Moins will have to wait. I have too much to do. I will come back for you, I promise. Wait for me!"

"But —" she said, sounding confused. "How —"

"Good-bye!"

Turning, I jogged up the darkening trail after my brother. We still had a long way to go . . . and prisoners to deliver to the dungeon.

Fifty feet from the sea, Queen Moins' song abruptly ceased.

Conner wasn't moving fast, and it didn't take me long to catch up with him on the road. Stubbornly, he still refused to ride Apollo.

"You're only slowing us down!" I protested.

"Then I'll walk faster," he growled back.

And for a short time, he actually managed it.

The hour was not terribly late when we finally did reach Castle Amber. Oil lanterns hanging over the gates and in the courtyard provided plenty of light.

Stableboys came racing out when they heard the clatter of hoofs on flagstones. They drew up short when they saw Conner (covered in blood from head to heel, still bleeding from his head wound), Isadora (bound and gagged and struggling faintly to free herself as she lay across my horse's back), and me (tired and dirty and almost as covered with blood as Conner). We made quite a spectacle.

I bellowed for the captain of the guard. Thirty seconds later, a barefoot Captain Yoon dashed from the guardhouse, swordbelt in hand and nightclothes flapping on his back. He must have been deeply asleep.

"Highness!" He saluted, expression growing ever more alarmed as he took in all the blood. "What happened?"

"Sorry to wake you, Captain." I chuckled humorlessly. "We were attacked on the beach. We left two survivers behind — they're wounded badly enough that they won't be going anywhere fast. Send a patrol out to collect them. I want them locked in the dungeon until we have time to question them properly."

"Yes, Sire!" He saluted again, then jogged back to the guardhouse, I assumed to finish getting dressed. He was a good man; I could count on him to handle everything quickly and efficiently.

That just left Conner and Isadora.

"You there!" I motioned for the closest stableboy. Gulping, he darted forward and bowed.

"Yes, S-sire?"

"Get the blacksmith out of bed. I need chains, and I need them now. Go!"

"Yes, Sire!" He turned and ran.

I returned to Conner. Though we had taken it slowly, I could tell that the long walk had nearly gotten the better of him. He swayed and had to steady himself against the stable wall.

"Want a chair?" I asked.

"I'm fine! Stop being a pest!"

Just then Freda appeared at my side as if from thin air. "Is that Isadora?" she asked with a gasp, staring at my horse. "What happened?"

"She attacked us with a dozen men," I said. Quickly, I summarized the fight. "Conner's the one to be concerned about." I nodded toward our brother. "He's took a nasty slice to the head. I was about to call for the barber."

"Does he need stitches?"

"Yes."

"Then I will take care of him."

She hurried to Conner, took his elbow, and steered him toward her quarters. She spoke quietly in his ear: "It will hurt, and quite a lot, but —" and they vanished inside.

I laughed to myself. My family had the worst bedside manners.

Then the blacksmith arrived, and I explained what I wanted done to Isadora: shackles on her legs and arms, an iron hood of some kind over her head, and a metal gag that could be removed when we wanted to feed her. I had no idea how long it would take Dad and Freda to cure her. If Aber tried to contact her with a Trump before they finished, I didn't want her speaking with him.

The smith nodded gravely when I finished.

"It will be done, Sire," he promised.

"When? Tonight?"

"I will start at once."

"Good. And take care — even wounded, she's more than capable of killing you and all the castle guards. Keep her subdued at all times. You might want to start with leg and arm restraints, just to make certain."

Without another word, I headed for my father's workshop. If Aber really *had* done something to her, we needed to undo it, and fast. One less psychotic warrior after my head would be a welcome change!

And, after that, I wanted the long, hot soak in a tub I'd prescribed for Conner, followed by the same thick slab of steak and half a dozen bottles of wine.

Dad insisted on dragging me back down to the blacksmith's shop while he examined her. The smith had already fastened short, heavy chains around her arms and legs; she could barely move. He was working on an eyeless mask to cover the whole of her face. It had a tiny slit for a mouth . . . just enough to feed her.

"Do you think it will keep Aber from contacting her with a Trump?" I asked Dad.

"Yes." He nodded. "He might sense her being alive, but he will not be able to reach her."

"Good."

Dad had brought an ivory-inlaid walnut box. He set it next to the spot where Isadora sat, motioning for the guards to back up. They did so. Then he flipped back the lid, revealing a case lined with red velvet. Inside sat several large, smoke-colored crystals, each as long as my hand. He selected one, removed Isadora's blindfold, and peered into her eyes. She blinked and glared at us both the whole time. If she hadn't been gagged, I think she would have spat in his face.

"Interesting, interesting!" Dad muttered, turning his crystal.

"What do you see?" Unable to help myself, I leaned over his shoulder. "Is she under a spell or not?"

"There is a *geas* laid upon her," he said, rising. He pronounced it "gash." "Maybe two or three. It looks like Aber's handiwork."

"Not Swayvil's?"

"I think not. The *geas* is effective, but clumsy in its execution. Swayvil is not clumsy."

I nodded slowly. "Is that some kind of spell?"

"Yes . . . a compulsion, in other words. Isadora cannot help herself. She must obey its command."

"Kill me?" I asked.

"That would be a good guess, yes."

I hesitated. "You said there might be two or three," I said. "What would the others do?"

"You tell me. Has she been doing anything strange or unusual . . . perhaps out-of-character?"

"Well . . . she *has* been following Aber's orders like a trained lap-dog, even when her own military training — not to mention logic! —

would have told her to do things differently."

"Then another *geas* may involve Aber. Perhaps it makes her love or trust him . . . or worship him as a god."

I shrugged. "Any of those would fit."

Dad packed up his crystal. "We will never know exactly what each *geas* made her do. That is not how they work."

"Can you remove it . . . *them*?"

He laughed. "Aber thinks far too highly of his work. *Of course* I can remove them. But perhaps I can offer a better solution."

"What?"

"If I alter each *geas* slightly, they may work to our advantage. What if Isadora worships *you* instead of Aber? What if she wants him dead at any cost? You can let her kill him for you. Rest assured, she will be more thorough than you were when it comes to destroying his body!"

The idea shocked and appalled me. "How can you even suggest doing that to your own daughter?" I demanded. "If I accepted, I would be no better than Aber!"

He shrugged, his smile lopsided, like Aber's. "Sometimes, my boy, I think you are not ruthless enough to be a king. Given the chance, Swayvil would have done it. Aber *did* do it. Tit for tat."

"Just remove the *geas*," I said in a cold voice. "I don't care if there are one or ten of them. I will not leave any family members under spells."

I had a feeling Isadora would prove a useful and loyal friend once freed from Aber.

Dad shrugged. "As you wish, my boy. It *is* your head."

"How long will it take you?"

"I should finish by dawn, if I am left alone."

Excellent. I nodded slowly. We might not need a metal hood for Isadora after all.

I asked, "Are you sure you don't need help?"

"I am certain. Go have drinks with Lord Dire, or bother Freda and your brother. Let me work in peace!"

I shrugged. "Fair enough."

Rising, I headed into the castle. Plots and plans turned through my head, a thousand different scenarios and possible outcomes. *Aber . . . the swords of Iccarion . . . King Swayvil . . . Lord Dire . . . the Feynim . . .*

I still had many loose ends to tie up.

TWENTY-THREE

By the time I located them in one of the sitting rooms, Freda had already cleaned, stitched, and bandaged Conner's head. Washed up and dressed in clean clothes once more, my brother looked almost normal as he sipped red wine and nibbled on a tea biscuit.

"Feeling better?" I asked.

"Yep!" He raised his goblet to Freda. "You can't ask for a better doctor."

Freda made light of it, but I could tell she enjoyed the praise.

I sat, then told them what Dad had discovered about Isadora. They nodded solemnly until I mentioned his offer to change the spells rather than remove them.

Freda looked distinctly unsettled. "He should never have suggested that," she said. "It is . . . wrong in many, many ways. It goes against one of the great unwritten laws of Chaos. We must never control one another this way . . . nor, discovering such control, allow it to continue."

"Aber did it."

"Aber is an abomination. As I told you, he must be destroyed."

"Yes," I agreed. That was becoming abundantly clear to me.

"Dad is the real bastard here!" Conner fumed, face growing red with anger. "Someone ought to lay a *geas* on him!"

"Maybe politeness?" I suggested.

"Or table manners?" he countered.

"Honesty!"

"Personal hygiene!"

We both laughed.

"Humility would serve him better," Freda said darkly. "Leave him to his work, Oberon. But do not trust him. He and Aber are more alike than you yet realize."

I nodded slowly. Aber had indeed inherited many of Dad's traits.

"Now," Freda said more lightly, "I have had a chance to discuss our problems more fully with Lord Dire."

Conner and I exchanged a glance. What did *that* mean?

"And," Freda continued, "after much consideration, the Dires have agreed to a new betrothal ceremony."

"Oh, no you don't —" I began.

"Della Dire," she said loudly, drowning out my voice, "has agreed to marry Conner."

I blinked in surprise. "What!"

"Really?" Conner grinned. "That's great news! I accept!"

"It makes the best of a bad situation," she said severely, shaking her head at both of us. "But we all believe it is for the best. Our family will be allied with the Dires after all. And Della swears she loves him. Conner, you *do* feel some affection for her as well?"

"I do!" Conner vowed. "Thank you, Freda . . . this is the best news I've had in months!"

She nodded. "We will hold the betrothal ceremony tomorrow

night. The wedding will take place six months later."

I raised my cup. "To the happy couple! May you never regret your doom, Conner!"

Late that night, as I lay in bed with the day's events running through my mind, Freda's comment about Dad and Aber being alike came back to me. True, they both served their own purposes. True, I had never quite known where their loyalties lay. But would Dad betray me, given a chance to advance his own agenda? I didn't think so.

But, as the saying goes, I wouldn't have bet my kingdom on it. I would watch him more carefully in the future.

One of the things any soldier learns over the years is to grab as much rest as you can whenever you can. I closed my eyes, slept long and deep, and dreamed pleasantly of Iccarion's sword, *King-maker*, mine now.

A pleasant dream, finally. I clung to it.

When I woke the next morning, I found myself mentally sharp and clear-headed. It might have only been five or six hours of sleep, but I felt greatly restored. My leg had completely healed. My other aches and pains had vanished. I could have taken on an army of Isadoras!

Rising, I hurried through my morning ablutions. Isadora should be cured by now, if all went well. The Dires would be satisfied with Della marrying Conner. Everything seemed to be coming together nicely.

Whistling cheerfully, I dressed and went down to breakfast. To-day, I wouldn't even mind if Lady Dire hissed at me.

I seemed to be the first one up. The kitchen staff was still setting out the breakfast dishes. I helped myself to a selection of eggs and meats, then sat down and ate.

Halfway through the meal, Conner joined me. He was still grinning happily.

"Don't get *too* happy," I said. "You aren't married yet. And I have big plans for today."

"Let me guess. You're planning a party for me after the betrothal ceremony?"

"Not exactly." I laughed. "After breakfast, we're going to kill Aber!"

"What!" he cried. "How?"

"With Isadora. You'll see." I grinned. "Eat up!"

An hour later, in the library, I raised Aber's Trump and studied his face. In a few seconds my brother answered. Once more his image wavered; he must be far away . . . still in the Courts of Chaos?

"Oberon." His eyes narrowed slightly, but his face showed no emotions this time. If my call had taken him by surprise, he didn't show it. "As always, a pleasure. Would you like to see a new trick?"

"If you've learned to bleed on command, sure."

"Very funny."

I looked over his shoulder. As before, he sat in an artist's workshop, complete with drawing table, paintbrushes, and jars of pigment. Casually, he threw a cloth over something he had been painting. I couldn't see what it was, but I assumed it would eventually mean trouble for me.

"I need a favor," I said.

"I'm out of glue. Just in case someone is trying to cut off *your* head."

"Very funny. Take a look at this."

I reached to one side and dragged Isadora into his line of sight. With her arms tied behind her back, a gag in her mouth, and heavy iron shackles on her legs, she looked particularly pathetic. The cuts and bruises on her face and arms had already begun to heal, but yellow-black and crusted with dried blood, they looked far worse than they really were.

Chuckling, I said, "I believe this belongs to you."

Even tied up, Isadora showed plenty of spirit. Glaring fiercely at me, she struggled to work her hands loose. It wouldn't work, though; I had double-checked everything.

Aber looked from Isadora to me and back again.

"I'm surprised you didn't kill her," he said.

"She didn't betray me. She never pretended to be my friend. An honest enemy must be respected. Unlike, say, *you*."

"Get on with it," Aber snarled. "What do you want, Oberon?"

"I need one particular Trump, and I know you have it."

"Paint your own. Or get Dad to do it for you. I'm through helping; you're all on your own."

"Shut up and listen, Aber. I need that Trump, and I need it badly. Today. Right now, in fact. And I know it's one you already have."

"Go hang yourself," he said, "and I'll consider it."

"I'll make it worth your while. I'll trade you Isadora for it."

He paused. I could tell my bait intrigued him.

Our sister continued to glare at me with a hatred so intense, it bordered on insane. Chuckling, I tickled her under the chin.

Aber leaned forward. "Obviously you're a better fighter than she is. Why should I take her back? I don't need a failed second-rate warrior."

I shrugged. "She must be the only person in our whole family who's still on friendly terms with you. That's got to be worth something."

"Maybe a little," he admitted.

I knew then that I had him. I tried not to smirk.

"Anyway," I said, "I have no use for her, and our numbers have dwindled down enough that I don't want to kill any more family members if I don't have to. If you'll promise to keep her away from me, I'll trade her back to you."

"Okay. Send her through." He reached toward her.

"Not so fast!" I said sharply. "Like I said, I want a Trump first."

"Which one?"

"Uh-uh. I'm not telling you. Throw me your deck. I'll take three Trumps — including the one I want. By the time you figure out which one I need, I'll be finished with it. I don't want you trying to kill me again."

He stared at me for a long time as if debating the wisdom of accepting my offer. Which Trump did I want so desperately? It had to be driving him crazy.

"What's the catch?" he asked.

"There isn't any," I said. "Three Trumps of my choice for Isadora. And I won't even cut off her head first."

I glanced her way, and she gave me a glare that would have frozen a lake. I laughed. Well played.

"All right," Aber said. "I agree."

"Throw me your deck, then. Like I said, I'll take three and give the rest back. With Isadora."

Aber looked at Isadora. "Is he telling the truth?" he asked.

She gave him a sullen half nod.

"Very well," he said smothly. He drew a pouch from his belt and threw it to me. "Pick your cards. And make sure it's only three — not a single one more!"

"I am a man of my word," I said severely.

I went through his Trumps one at a time. Some showed weirdly colored landscapes or strangely furnished rooms. I recognized very few of them. And the people! Half-squids, giants with horned heads, men with three eyes or six arms . . . monsters, all.

Conner moved closer and peeked over my shoulder.

"That one, I think," he said, as I came to one showing a richly appointed room decorated in shades of red and gray. Tapestries on the wall showed dragons battling an army of almost-men; low red couches offered a place to sit. Could it be some sort of antechamber in the palace?

I nodded and removed it.

"And this one." I pulled out a Trump showing Isadora. No telling when I'd need it. Then I took a random card . . . which turned out to be a street scene somewhere in the Courts of Chaos. The sky was full of swirling colors; the street was crowded. Let Aber try to figure out which of the three I really needed . . . assuming he lived that long!

I tucked my new Trumps away, returned the others to their pouch, and tossed them all back to Aber. He bobbled the pouch, then dropped it. His coordination seemed off; perhaps my killing him had something to do with it.

"And here is payment," I said, yanking Isadora forward by her chains. "She's all yours. Let me unchain her for you first . . ."

That's when Conner swung up his crossbow and pointed it straight at Isadora's heart. He played it perfectly, too.

"Don't do anything stupid," he told her. "You may be faster and stronger than I am, but you know I won't miss at this range."

"Idiot." Though badly muffled by her gag, I still heard the word clearly enough to understand.

Aber smirked.

"Shut up," Conner said. "You're the one who lost, Isadora. Follow Dad's example. Run away and don't come back. The next time you attack us, you won't live to regret it."

She didn't deign to reply.

I unfastened the shackles around her ankles, then drew my knife and slit the ropes binding her wrists behind her back. She began to massage her hands, trying to get her circulation flowing again.

"Go on." I gave her a hard shove toward Aber. "If you ever attack me again," I said coldly, "you won't get off so lightly. I never forget an insult."

Gently now, Aber reached out for her. She took his hand, and he drew her into his workshop.

Then Conner swung his crossbow around to cover our brother.

"You just made the worst bargain of your life," Aber told me, grinning madly.

"I don't think so," I said. Over his shoulder, I watched Isadora pick up an empty easel. Slowly she raised it over her head.

"What do you mean?" he demanded.

"Look behind you."

He glanced over his shoulder. He only had a second to scream before Isadora smashed his head in . . . and our connection was lost.

*   *   *

"What do you think she's going to do to him?" Conner asked.

"What would *you* do if you found out he'd had you secretly under his control for months or maybe even years, making you kill people for him? And then you finally got him alone in a room?"

"You know," he said, "I almost feel sorry for him!"

"He's only getting what he deserves."

"I did say *almost.*"

I picked up the Trumps I'd taken from Aber. I studied the one with the room lightly, letting my consciousness expand just enough to know the chamber it showed lay empty . . . or at least the portion of it depicted in the card. If our luck held, Conner and I would get into the King of Chaos's palace undetected.

Then would come the hard part . . . finding that sword, *Kingmaker.* And anything else that might prove valuable and useful to Amber's continued existence!

TWENTY-FOUR

n hour earlier, over breakfast, I had confided in Conner my plans to kill Aber and steal King Swayvil's sword. I had never wanted anything in my life as much as I wanted *King-maker*. It was more than a mere wish. I *had* to have it. The future of Amber itself depended on it.

"Why bother?" he said. "Lord Dire's sword is pretty enough, but you can find a thousand nicer ones in Shadow if you poke around a little."

"You don't understand . . . there's something about it. Ever since I held *Baryn-killer* and heard the story of its creation, I haven't been able to get it out of my mind. I *have* to have one of Iccarion's swords. And I want Swayvil's!"

He frowned. "Lord Dire's would probably be easier to take. Not that I'd recommend it! And he would be less likely to send all the armies of Chaos after you to get it back."

"Taking *Baryn-killer* is not an option." The Dires would be family as soon as Della married Conner, and I wouldn't steal from them just to suit my whims. Besides, according to my vision, I was meant to have *King-maker*. "If I take Swayvil's, at least I'll feel as though I've accomplished something. Tweaked his nose for all the trouble he's caused us. And if the sword means half as much to him as I think it does, perhaps he'll feel the loss as keenly as we've felt ours."

Conner sighed. "I assume you have a plan?"

"Yes. And if it works, he'll never know who took it!"

Then I had explained how we would trick Aber in taking Isadora back in exchange for the Trump that would get us into Swayvil's palace.

"And Isadora will kill Aber for us," I concluded. "She'll have her revenge. Aber will be dead once and for all. I'll have *King-maker*. Everyone will be happy!"

"Brilliant!" Conner said admiringly.

"But will it work?" I said. I thought so. But if he saw any problems, I wanted to know about them.

He shoved back his chair and stood. "Let's see if Dad is finished. I know Isadora will be game to help if she's free of the *geas*."

Now I raised the Trump I had taken from Aber's deck and stared at the image of the room. Slowly it came to life, but in an odd and flickery sort of way, as if our worlds didn't quite mesh properly. As nearly as I could tell, it was deserted.

We had no time for hesitation: our little raid had to be carried out quickly to work. Swayvil would never expect us to strike within his palace. That was our one great advantage.

I took Conner's arm and pulled him forward with me, into the chamber. It was just as the card depicted: tapestries on the walls showing scenes of dragons fighting each other, and a scattering of furniture: oddly-shaped wooden chairs, a plush red sofa, a low oval table. Heavy red-and-gold carpets covered the floor.

And it was empty. Finally, a stroke of good luck!

As I stood looking around, a wave of dizziness swept through me, followed by nausea. The floor seemed to slide under my feet. I staggered.

"Easy!" Conner said, steadying my arm.

"I just need to get used to it again . . ." I muttered.

It had been far worse the first time I had come to the Courts of Chaos — I had passed out for three days, and my father finally used magic to wake me. Even so, it had taken several more days for me to get my "Chaos legs" as Aber had called it.

For now, I could put up with a bit of dizziness and discomfort. As long as I didn't pass out, I would be fine. It shouldn't last more than a few minutes this time.

"Here . . . take this one."

I handed him Aber's Trump, which he tucked away with his own deck. I wished I still had my own set of Trumps.

Conner wandered through the room, picking up small objects I couldn't readily identify, then setting them back. I trailed him. And, slowly, my vision grew steady. It hadn't taken more than a few minutes this time.

"I think I'm ready," I said. "Where do you think we are? Aber's rooms?"

"Must be. There isn't anything personal in this room, though. Clearly he hasn't been living here."

"At least it's safe," I said. "Any guess how far Swayvil's rooms will be?"

"I have no idea. But we must be about as far from them as you can get."

"What makes you think so?"

"If *you* were the King of Chaos, would *you* put Aber in the suite next to *your* bedroom?"

"Good point." Our brother had betrayed so many people, I wouldn't let him anywhere near the place I slept!

"So," I mused aloud, "we have to get out of here, cross the whole of the palace undetected, find Swayvil's private quarters, and rob him while he sleeps."

Conner grinned. "This *is* a crazy plan, isn't it?"

"And the best way to do it . . ." I closed my eyes, concentrating on Swayvil's face and body, and in a few seconds the transformation was complete. Sometimes it helped to be a shapeshifter. I now looked exactly like the king of Chaos the last time I had seen him.

Raising my hands, I studied my new, slightly darker, slightly more wrinkled skin, with its faintly serpentine look. Yes, it would do.

Conner studied me critically. "Not bad," he said. "But you'll never fool anyone in the palace."

"What's wrong?" I prided myself on my shape-changing abilities and felt vaguely insulted. "Tell me and I'll fix it."

"It's the clothes," he said. He waved at my whole outfit. "Swayvil would never dress like *that*."

I glanced down. He had a point — my physical appearance mattered, but the real king of Chaos would never be seen in public wearing a plain linen shirt and pants, along with a common soldier's boots.

Hastily I looked around the room, but I saw nothing remotely resembling a closet or wardrobe. Not that Swayvil would keep his robes of state in Aber's quarters . . .

"So — where do we go next?" I asked helplessly. Back to Amber? Of course the castle tailor could always make me something, but Old Jed had a reputation for quality of workmanship rather than speed. . . .

"I'll take care of it. I knew you brought me along for a reason, though I didn't think it was to be your valet!"

He reached out into the air, felt around for a second, then plucked a bundle of clothing out of nothingness . . . that Logrus trick again. For the millionth time, I wished I could do it, too.

"Here," and he shoved it into my hands. "Put these on."

I untied the bundle and found deep red robes with rubies sewn along the hem. Around the collar, silver and gold thread made a checkerboard pattern.

Quickly, I changed clothes, and then tossed my old ones behind the sofa. Hopefully no one would find them anytime soon.

"Better?" I asked.

Conner slowly me circled, studying my disguise. Finally he nodded.

"It will do," he said.

I began to relax. Maybe it wouldn't be so hard after all.

"Now you just need to fix your face," he said.

"What! Did I do it wrong?"

"Yes — it's all wrong."

I touched my chin, cheeks, and forehead — all creased in the right places — and patted my short, bristly gray hair. Everything seemed in order. Had I missed something? I chewed my lower lip thoughtfully.

"What do I need to change, exactly?"

"Your face. You look entirely too smug and happy. That won't do at all if you're going to impersonate Swayvil. You need to get *angry*. Or at least mildly annoyed. Remember, he scowls a lot. Never smile — unless someone is about to die. The one time I saw him really enjoying himself was at a public execution."

I frowned, trying to figure out how to change my expression to match. As I did, he nodded.

"Much better. I think you've got it!"

"What about you?" I asked.

"I'm not much good at shape-shifting. Besides, who's going to tell King Swayvil he can't bring whoever he wants into the palace? Treat me like an honored guest and no one will ask what I'm doing here."

"All right. Then let's go!"

I stepped quickly to the large, ornately carved door. It had to lead into a hallway. The faster we moved, the greater our chances of success. In and out . . . a lightning-fast raid, then back to Amber.

Where would Swayvil keep *King-maker*? In his private rooms, I guessed. If not there, though, where else might it be? The armory?

When I touched the doorknob, a face suddenly knotted up in the middle of the door. Its brow furrowed; its lips skinned back in an angry grimace.

"Who are you, and how did you get inside this room?" it demanded.

TWENTY-FIVE

I drew up short. Dad had designed doors similar to this one in his house in the Beyond. They had been frustratingly loyal at times, and frustratingly stupid at others.

"Don't you recognize me?" I demanded. Might as well bluff it through. If a door wouldn't open for the king of Chaos, it wouldn't open at all.

It squinted up at me. Hopefully it wouldn't ask for a password.

"No, I don't recognize you. Who are you? "

"I'm the king. Now open up before I have you chopped to kindling!"

"Begging your pardon, Highness, but I would be a poor excuse for a door if I believed everyone who came along claiming to be the king. It's happened a hundred times if it's happened once! For all I know, you might be an assassin!"

True enough; there were many shapeshifters in Chaos. But other than my face, what else would possibly convince this door to let us through?

I said, "I got in here because my friend and loyal subject Aber gave me a Trump."

I held it up. The door squinted.

"Yes, I see," it said. "That's my room, all right. And I do recognize

Master Aber's fine workmanship. He is a genius, you know. He told me so himself!"

"He would not have given it to me if he didn't want me to use it, right?"

"Perhaps."

"And aren't your instructions to keep people *out*, not *in*?"

"Perhaps. And the man with you is . . . ?"

I glanced at Conner, who folded his arms and stared at the door impassively. With the sword at his side, he looked like a soldier.

"A bodyguard, of course."

The face frowned for a moment, thinking.

"Very well, Highness. Your arguments have swayed me." The face began to melt back into the wood. A second later, the lock clicked and the door swung open. "You can't be too careful these days . . ."

I glanced at Conner. "Ready?"

"Let's get it over with!"

I stepped into the hallway . . . and drew up short.

Walking toward me, a pair of trident-carrying guards in tow, came Queen Moins herself.

I gulped. What was *she* doing here? I didn't know whether to duck back inside the room or try to bluff it out. And I didn't get a chance to decide; she had already spotted me and quickened her step. I would have to greet her.

I scowled unhappily. According to Conner, that's what the real Swayvil would have done anyway.

"Queen Moins," I said in greeting, lowering my voice an octave to match Swayvil's growl.

"King Swayvil. I am delighted to finally catch you."

"Walk with me," I said.

I started up the corridor at a brisk pace, as if I had an important appointment to get to. Conner followed five feet behind me, joining Moins' bodyguards.

"Is everything to your liking?" I asked.

"Everyone has been quite attentive, thank you." She swallowed. Something must have been bothering her.

"Go on," I said bluntly. "You have something to say. Spit it out."

She looked me in the eye. "The answer is no."

"No!" I echoed. *But what was the question?*

"I have considered well your most generous offer, King Swayvil," she continued a moment later, "But my lands are my own, and I cannot put them under your banner no matter what you offer."

"Will you reconsider?" I asked. "I make a powerful ally. And an even more powerful enemy."

She halted. "Do not threaten me, Swayvil."

"You like him, don't you?" I demanded. There had to be a reason she wouldn't throw in with the king of Chaos.

She looked startled. "Who?"

"That whelp Oberon, of course!"

"I found him refreshingly honest," she replied. "Which is more than can be said for you or your ministers."

She paused, and I stopped too, regarding her with a measure of new-found interest. She liked me!

"What are you smiling about?" she demanded. "Is this some game for you?"

"Just a stray thought. Continue, Queen Moins. And your feelings about Oberon are . . . ?"

"What feelings I have are my own," she snapped. "I am returning to Caer Beatha. Do not summon me here again!"

Turning, she strode angrily back the way we had come. I glanced at Conner and shrugged slightly.

"I take it you know her?" he said.

"She rules the undersea city, Caer Beatha."

"Well, you *are* looking for a new wife . . ." he said. "She's a bit old, but you might be able to make it work if —"

I punched him in the arm. Hard.

"Hey!" he said.

"Get back to our business," I said sharply. "We have to find Swayvil's quarters."

The hallway ended at another, broader corridor that bustled with people. Most appeared to be servants carrying supplies to the kitchens or wheeling carts laden with dishes. We must be near the dining hall . . . not where we wanted to be at all. For all I knew, Swayvil himself might be eating.

Servants began bowing to me and clustering around. I waved them away.

"Back to work with you!"

"Yes, Highness!" they cried.

"Wait!" I said, pointing to a man with red skin and three short horns growing out of his forehead. He had a tray piled high with some sort of lumpy blue-green fruits. I'd get him to show me the way to my quarters. "I want that tray brought to my rooms. Now."

"Of course, Highness!"

He turned up the hallway we had just come down, and I trailed him. Let the servants think I had come to get a snack.

Half a dozen turns later, we reached a more opulently furnished hallway. The lamp sconces gleamed with solid gold; the doors to either side gleamed with gold and silver inlay. And there were guards at either end, hell-creatures with their snake-scaled skin and bright red eyes. They wore ceremonial uniforms, with silvered breastplates, red-plumed helms, and polished black boots.

Snapping to attention as I passed, they stared straight at me. I tried to frown more severely. This would be the biggest test of my impersonation so far. These creatures must see me every day. If I could fool them . . . if I could make it through Swayvil's bedroom door . . .

The servant halted before a set of double-doors with a guard stationed to either side. One of them reached over, turned the knob, and swung the door inward. The servant carried his tray inside, and I followed with Conner right behind.

The guards said not a word.

We were in some sort of sitting room, with low tables and richly padded chairs. A diffuse light came from an intricate set of panels set into the walls near the ceiling . . . probably magical. Tapestries lining two of the walls showed intricate geometric patterns; the patterns moved constantly like serpents, weaving in and out.

Then, from somewhere ahead, came the tinny notes of some many-stringed instrument. The melody reminded me faintly of Queen Moins song, but rendered discordant and ugly. Did Swayvil keep a musician in his rooms? I frowned. I hadn't planned on anyone else being in here.

"Put the tray there," I said, pointing to one of the low table. "Then go."

"Yes, Highness." The servant set it down, bowed, then left without another word. The guards shut the door behind him. Conner and I were alone.

My brother sagged into a chair. His face was pale and his hands shook a little. He gulped air. A panic attack?

"Are you all right?" I demanded softly, kneeling beside him.

"Just nerves. I'm not as brave as you. When I saw those guards, I thought we were dead!"

"We're going to get away with it." I clasped his shoulder and gave him a reassuring grin. And it was true: I *knew* we were going to succeed. For once, everything had gone better than I ever could have hoped. "Keep watch here. I'm going to check out the other rooms."

I went into the next room, which turned out to be a library or study. Bookcases lined each wall from floor to ceiling, each shelf crammed so full with books, scrolls, and other papers that it would have been difficult to add anything. It made my father's library look empty in comparison.

A reading table sat in the middle of the room. On it, spread out for careful study, lay a set of blueprints . . . very familiar blueprints. With a jolt of panic, I recognized the full plans for Castle Amber . . . and *these* pages had some remarkable differences from the ones I remembered approving.

The west tower had markings identifying places where construction materials had been deliberately weakened. A chill ran through me as I read them. The tower's collapse had been carefully planned . . . the storm had not been responsible. This conspiracy had to include not only our architects, but our masons and other workers.

I paged through more of the blueprints, discovering secret passages into the dungeons and the south tower. Dad had mentioned catching several spies. This must be how they had been gaining entry into Castle Amber.

I debated taking these plans with me, but their disappearance would alert Swayvil as to who had been here. No one but a spy from Amber would be interested in them. No, it was better for me to leave them here. The mystery of who had stolen his sword would be enough.

When I got home, I would question the architects. They would reveal every change made to the castle without my permission. And, when I finished, their heads would hang over the gates as an example to every other worker. None would dare to work for Swayvil again.

I went into the next room . . . an immense chamber that housed Swayvil's bed as well as his collections of art and weapons.

The bed was a high, canopied platform. A dozen thick iron rings were set into the headboard, and chained to the rings lay a half dozen naked women, their bodies covered with bruises, half-healed cuts, open sores, and whip marks. They ranged in age from perhaps twelve or thirteen to their early twenties. They began to moan and writhe as they saw me.

"Stop that and be quiet," I snapped.

Instantly they shut up. I wasn't here for them; I had to find my sword. And yet I couldn't just leave them . . .

After a moment's hesitation, I drew my knife and tossed it onto the bed. Perhaps one of them would have the courage to use it on Swayvil the next time he wanted to entertain himself in here.

I crossed to the racks of weapons and began examining swords carefully. From the gaudy to the elegant . . . from the flashy to the plain . . . he had weapons of every shape and size imaginable. It was by far the finest collection I had ever seen. Hundreds, perhaps thousands of blades hung there, ranging in size and shape from heavy long-swords to short, curved scimitars of a design like nothing I had ever seen before. I could have spent hours going through them all, admiring one then another, trying them all out.

I saw none like Lord Dire's *Baryn-killer*, however. None were as brilliantly decorated, as eye-drawingly beautiful, as Iccarion's sword.

Stepping back, I surveyed the rest of the room. Tables, tapestries, armoire, washstand . . . where would he keep his most valuable weapon?

My gaze settled on a wooden case on top of the armoire. Maybe there . . . ?

Eagerly I hurried over and lifted it down. The case, made of a dark wood, had a simple latch. I thumbed it open.

The breath caught in my throat. Inside, nested in a tray of red velvet made specifically to hold it, lay Iccarion's sword, *King-maker*. The long steel blade glistened faintly with a fresh coat of oil.

Slightly less ornate than *Baryn-killer*, *King-maker* was clearly a weapon meant to be used. Three large jewels decorated the hilt, a giant emerald in the pommel and two large diamonds in the guard. A scattering of pearls and smaller diamonds surrounded them.

Slowly, reverently, I eased it from the box. *Beautiful*. Slipping my hand around the handle, I raised it over my head, and I knew destiny had been fulfilled. The sword weighed almost nothing, and yet a strange thrill of power went through my arm and into my body.

I glanced at the bed. The knife I had tossed there had already disappeared, and none of the chained women would look in my direction. Yes, Swayvil would have quite a surprise the next time he went to sleep!

I couldn't just stand here gloating. Swayvil might come back at any time. Without a word to the women, I hurried back to the library, then into the sitting room.

Conner was gone. Either he had used a Trump to leave or he had gone into the hallway. If he had used a Trump, he had stranded me here . . . I hadn't replaced my own deck since losing them in the sea.

Cautiously I pulled open the door . . . and found Conner struggling in the hall against the two huge, burly guards with snake-scaled faces. They held my brother's arms in vicelike grips.

And, standing directly in front of me, stood King Swayvil himself.

I had caught everyone by surprise. Without hesitation, I leaped forward and placed the tip of my sword to Swayvil's throat.

"Let him go!" I said.

He returned my stare, but seemed to have no real fear of me.

"You must be Oberon," he said. "Your brother told me you would be coming." He chuckled. It was a thoroughly evil sound.

I swallowed. Which brother . . . Conner? Or Aber?

Swayvil's gaze fell to *King-maker* in my hand. "I see you have found Iccarion's sword. Excellent, is it not? *Feel* its power in your hand. Yes . . . take it! I make it a gift! Take it and go while you still may!"

"Tell your men to release my brother."

He glanced toward the guards and gave a short nod. They let go of Conner's arms, and he ran to my side.

"Send your men into your quarters," I said to Swayvil.

Again, he nodded. Both guards filed inside, casting hard glances my way. They would have liked nothing better than to tear my head off.

"You next," I said to Swayvil, motioning with *King-maker*.

He also went inside. I pulled the door shut.

Conner fumbled out his Trumps, raised one showing his bedroom in Castle Amber, and stared at it. After a moment, he lowered it again. Sweat began to bead on his forehead.

"Something is blocking it," he said with dismay. "We can't use our Trumps here!"

Damn Swayvil's magic. I tried the door, but he had locked it from inside. At the sound of my hand on the knob, I heard mocking laughter. Well, I'd have a laugh of my own when he tried to bed those women!

Somewhere close, a gong began to ring. An alarm?

"Come on!" I said, starting up the corridor at a run. I kept my new sword out.

We headed back the way we had come. Aber's room might provide sanctuary. Maybe our Trumps would work there.

Then I remembered Queen Moins. Perhaps she would prove useful now. She obviously had powers different from our own. Which door had been hers?

I found the proper one, pounded on it, and a moment later it was opened by one of her servants. The man gaped at me as I shoved past him. Conner barred the door behind us.

"What is the meaning of this —" Queen Moins began.

I let Swayvil's appearance fall away. As Oberon, I turned and addressed the queen.

"Your Highness." I dropped to one knee before her and bowed my head. If I appealed to her sense of honor, she might help us. "We are being pursued. I know you have feelings for me. If you want me to live through this day, send me back to our world!"

Then I looked beseechingly up into her eyes. I saw conflicting emotions at war . . . fear . . . anger . . . and perhaps even love.

After a second, she took a pendant from around her neck and put it over my head.

"*Caer Beatha,*" she said, touching it.

The world grew cloudy, as though I gazed out through the bottom of a wine bottle. When I reached for Conner, my hand passed through his arm. Apparently Queen Moins hadn't included him in her spell.

"*No-o-o-o!*" I screamed.

TWENTY-SIX

n instant later, the room disappeared. I felt myself falling, a dazzling light surrounded me, and then I hit water flat on my back with a loud splash. I came up into sunlight, gasping for air. My back stung; the air had been knocked from my lungs. For several heartbeats I just floated, shaking my head and slowly treading water, supported for the moment by air trapped in my robes — though they were rapidly becoming waterlogged.

I had lost Conner. The realization hit me hard. I clung to the slim hope that Queen Moins would hide him from Swayvil. If she truly loved me, she would try to protect those I cared about, wouldn't she? And I cared a great deal about my brother.

At least our raid hadn't been a complete failure. I still held *Kingmaker.* . . .

Slowly I turned, looking for help. Not a boat in sight, not a man on the beach. I could see Castle Amber rising high in the distance, though. Almost home. I had a long, hard swim ahead of me.

My robes began to pull me beneath the waves. No sense putting it off. The longer I waited, the harder it would be to get ashore.

I took a deep breath and raised both arms, letting my body slide down into the water, out of the robes. Then I bent almost double and, with fumbling hands, cut the laces of my boots with *King-maker*. Freeing my feet helped a lot, but the clothes I had worn under the robes continued to drag on me like lead weights. My lungs were already burning for air. Without Queen Moins's magic in the water, I knew I wouldn't be able to breathe down here. I had to hurry. Quickly I kicked off my pants, and then I ripped away my shirt.

Sudden motion drew my eyes toward the sea's depths. I was thirty feet underwater at this point. I spotted a long white line below . . . the stairway to Caer Beatha? I couldn't see any of the city's buildings through the greenish murk, but I knew where it lay.

Apparently my arrival had not gone unnoticed. Dozens of warriors from Caer Beatha were swimming up towards me. They all carried tridents. From their angry expressions, I suspected their intentions weren't friendly.

I raised my head and began to kick toward the surface. I'd have to swim for shore as best I could. I'd be lucky to make it before they overtook me.

Twenty-five feet – twenty –

A huge shadow fell across the sea overhead, completely blotting out the sun. A great bulk settled onto the water, and giant scaled legs ending in claws as large as my whole body dipped through the water toward me.

What in the seven hells?

I drew up short, treading water to hold my position. My lungs ached fiercely. I had almost run out of air . . . and time. The tridentmen from Caer Beatha had almost reached me.

Some days, the gods have a perverse sense of humor.

Of course, it was a dragon sitting on the water directly overhead. I had the strangest feeling it was hungry . . . and waiting for me to bob to the surface!

HERE ENDS BOOK ONE OF
SHADOWS OF AMBER

THE STORY WILL CONCLUDE IN BOOK II,
SWORD OF CHAOS